MW01127695

PINEAPPLE

DISCO

A Pineapple Port Mystery: Book Six

Amy Vansant

ISBN- 1718850840
ISBN- 978-1718850842
Library of Congress: 1718850840

Vansant Creations, LLC / Amy Vansant
Annapolis, MD
http://www.AmyVansant.com
http://www.PineapplePort.com

Copy editing by Carolyn Steele.
Proofreading by Effrosyni Moschoudi & Connie Leap
Cover by Steven Novak

DEDICATION

To Gordon. I miss you every day.

CHAPTER ONE

It started with the brush of a hand.

Every day Gloria walked the River Walk, not far from her new beach apartment. After falling into a little money, she'd left the Pineapple Port retirement community for the cool beach breezes of the Gulf.

Gloria enjoyed nodding her head and smiling at the people who passed in the opposite direction when she walked. She liked everything about her new lifestyle by the water, but she especially enjoyed the walks.

Walking kept her need to *right wrongs* at bay.

She hadn't slashed a tire, or dropped a bug in a cocktail, or switched yard decorations between neighbors with competing gnome ideologies, in nearly three months.

Even Superman grew old and let a few offenses slide here and there, didn't he?

Gloria let her mind wander when she walked. She waved at dogs and called them *buddy,* or *sweetie* if they had a bow or a pink collar. She liked the Yorkie terrier with the watery eyes and the regal standard poodle that ran at the same graceful pace as her owner. The owner never smiled, but the dog's presence said she wasn't a bad person and Gloria believed the dog.

Thanks to the poodle, I let sourpuss off the hook. 'Old Gloria' never would have let that skinny woman's refusal to return a smile slide. I'm maturing.

Her patience had limits, of course. Gloria did *not* like the two ladies who hogged the whole sidewalk and never deigned to step aside for her to pass. *She* had to balance-beam the curb, or tumble into the bike lane to avoid being clipped by their stupid rounded shoulders. Those ladies...

Those ladies didn't deserve a pass.

After the fifth or sixth offense, Gloria followed them home. One had a New England Patriots football flag flying outside her house, so Gloria returned under cover of night to replace it with a Miami Dolphins flag. The next time she passed the women she made a point to *not* move out of their way. As they jostled to avoid knocking into her she shouted, "*Go Dolphins!*"

After that day, the women fell single file when they saw her coming. They knew *she* knew where they lived. Gloria had a giant bottle of vinegar for the other woman's manicured lawn, should they forget their manners.

See how she likes the word MOVE scrawled across her front yard in brown, dead grass.

Other than those two sidewalk-hogging, boorish wenches, Gloria liked the people and pets on her walk. She liked the chubby Italian man who waddled along yammering on his phone in his native tongue. She liked the woman who always wore too many clothes, but never appeared sweaty.

Classy.

Most of all, she liked the tanned man with the dark hair. He always flashed his perfect smile and winked. She didn't know if he wore dentures or had those replacement teeth people had drilled into their jaw bones, but his chompers were *impressive*. Nearly as striking as the cowlick in his magnificent mane of dark hair. The front row of follicles stood strong and proud, like a hair wave begging to be surfed.

I never properly appreciated men's hair until I grew older and suddenly none of the men have any. Think of all the hair I took for granted as a foolish young girl...

The man had kind eyes, and those sparkling orbs always found hers. At first, she'd thought the man was just friendly. After his walk she imagined he returned to a pretty wife sipping coffee on her lanai with a good book propped on her lap. But then she noticed he didn't wear a wedding ring. Not even the telltale tan line of a cheater. If he was a widower, he'd been one for some time.

The man's smile and wink were soon accompanied by a nod, the tip of an invisible hat, and once, what she felt sure was a blush.

Mornings changed. Gloria grew giddy pre-walk, eager to see Smiley Joe, which is what she'd started calling the man in her head.

Then it happened.

As she passed Smiley Joe on the narrow pathway, his hand brushed hers.

Gloria gasped and kept walking. After a dozen steps she glanced back, but Joe had continued on his way.

After that day, he *always* touched her hand. Anticipating the contact, her hand began to jerk away from her body, reaching to feel his, as if it had a mind of its own. Their touches became more eager. On day six their pinkies intertwined and uncoiled, slipping away like lovesick garden snakes as they continued in their opposite directions.

Then it happened. Smiley Joe wore his usual white t-shirt, but he'd handwritten *Hi* on the chest. She'd been so shocked to see the word she'd forgotten to reach for his hand.

Was that message for me?

The next day he wore a new t-shirt. She assumed it was new—it had looked as though the previous day's *Hi* was written in permanent marker and she couldn't imagine how he could have washed it out.

Now, his shirt said *Will.*

Gloria knew the messages on his shirts were for her. His eyes were playful. Twinkling with mischief.

He's a scamp.

On the third day, the shirt said *You.*

Gloria felt a rush of excitement.

It's a question! He's asking me a question on his shirt, one word per day.

The mornings became almost impossible to manage. She didn't want to leave too soon and miss meeting him at the spot they passed every day. She didn't know how far he walked before they met each other. Leave too soon and he might miss her entirely. Same applied to leaving too late. She had to wait until the exact right moment, 7:39 a.m. This grew increasingly difficult, because she kept waking up earlier and earlier, eager to see what his next word would be.

It was *Go.*

Hi Will You Go.

Gloria had new problems to consider. Would she recognize when the sentence was over? Would he remember to punctuate the last word with a question mark? Would the last tee feature *only* a question mark? And then what? If it was a question—and she assumed it was—how would she answer? Would she write it on *her* shirt with permanent marker? Should she go shopping for a cheap tee she didn't mind ruining with ink?

The next word was *Out.*

No punctuation.

Gloria didn't want to be presumptuous, but she felt confident she'd guessed the rest of his mysterious missive. Her day would soon arrive.

What if I accept his invitation and the message isn't for me?

If she wore a cheap tee with *Yes* written on it and he ignored her, she would just *die.*

The next day he smiled and winked with *With* on his tee. The day after that, *Me.*

Still no punctuation. She knew she had one more day. The question mark would be the next day. Or not. Maybe he'd forget to add punctuation.

Can I date a man who doesn't properly punctuate? So many questions...

Gloria drove to *Bealls* and bought a cheap white tee. It took nearly an hour to decide on the color of the marker. She'd had no idea they came in so many colors. Back in her day, permanent markers came in one color: black.

Period.

Or maybe red, too...but certainly not green and purple and...

She chose a feminine hot pink and hoped it didn't come off trashy.

She spent another two hours picking the size of the lettering and contemplating cursive versus block and all caps versus first letter capitalization only.

On Thursday, Smiley Joe walked by with a huge question mark on his shirt.

His other words had been in black, but the question mark glowed in hot pink, just like her *Yes* tee back home on her kitchen table.

It's as if we're meant to be together.

Gloria barely slept Thursday night. Her mind raced with anticipation and questions.

Should I add an exclamation point to the end of Yes? Would that be too forward?

Friday morning, she donned her block lettering, first-letter-cap, no punctuation, *Yes* tee and leapt from her car as if it were a circus cannon instead of a Mercedes. She adjusted her pace to keep from speed-walking to her destiny.

Gloria practiced holding people's gazes as she walked. She didn't want to hold Smiley Joe's attention too long and look desperate, but she didn't want him to wonder if her shirt was for him. Or maybe she did. If it seemed as if the question *hadn't* been for her, she wanted the opportunity to look away and keep walking, as if she always wore a tee with a giant pink *Yes* on it.

As she approached the portion of the walk where they always met, she could barely breathe.

It wasn't until she reached the corner that she realized he wasn't there.

She leaned forward, expecting to see him at any moment.

He never appeared.

On the drive back to her apartment, Gloria felt like a deflated balloon.

Where was he? Had he fallen ill? Twisted an ankle?

Maybe someone else had answered him?

No.

She *knew* the shirts had been for her.

After much hemming and hawing, she wore the *Yes* tee again the next day.

Again, he didn't show.

Something horrible had happened. Gloria was sure of it.

She needed a detective to find Smiley Joe.

She needed to call Charlotte.

CHAPTER TWO

Two Weeks Previous

Stephanie yawned into her hand and read the plaques on the wall of the bar for the fifth time.

Free beers tomorrow.

You can't drink all day if you don't start in the morning.

Wish you were beer.

She flicked a peanut across the bar top.

Nothing about this is right.

Assassins of her caliber weren't meant to spend time drinking terrible iced tea while watching teenagers peddle drugs on the corner.

This is Declan's fault.

She'd allowed herself to be inspired by her ex-boyfriend's inherently good nature. She missed him, and her usual charms had ceased to sway his affections her way. In an attempt to better resemble his *new* little Ms. Perfect Girlfriend, Charlotte, she'd decided to *pull a Dexter* and only kill people who deserved it.

It turned out being good was even more boring than she'd feared.

She'd *barely* refrained from killing the neighbor who reported her to her community association for not recycling. She was hiding behind the woman's bedroom door, knife in hand, when it hit her: *People aren't supposed to murder people for being bitchy.*

It was a close call. If the woman hadn't forgotten to brush her teeth Stephanie might have had to exterminate the tattle-telling little rat just to get out of the woman's rat-hole undetected.

No, she didn't trust her ability to identify *people who deserved to die* versus *people who are too annoying to live*, so she decided to pick a ham-handedly obvious target.

A drug dealer.

I should win some sort of serial killer Oscar for the restraint I've shown.

Not only was she hunting a drug dealer, but she was hunting the top banana. By sunrise, she could have easily taken out three or four of the hoppers on the corner, but she didn't. She could hear Declan in her head... *They probably had lousy home lives and fell in with the wrong crowd and blah blah bleeding heart blah...*

Stephanie knew Declan wouldn't give her any credit for killing a kid who made bad life choices.

She could have killed the slick-haired man who brought the corner kids their supply, but she didn't.

Instead, she decided next time the drop-off man showed up, she'd track *that* guy back to the biggest, *baddest* guy.

That meant a lot of surveillance; the most boring part of killing.

This is all my mother's fault.

Why did her mother have to pass down the serial killer gene? The time she wasted hunting, dreaming about hunting—she could have started a second business. Learned another language. Learned to cook soufflés...*something.*

The neighbor she nearly killed had a basket of knitting supplies. She'd stared at it for some time from her hiding spot behind the bedroom door. It seemed like such a peaceful hobby.

Why can't I love knitting?

Instead, she'd mulled using the knitting needle to kill the woman just to make her attack a little more sporting.

Maybe it wasn't *all* her mother's fault. Sure, her mother was the most prolific serial killer of all time—whether the world knew it or not—but her mother had also abandoned her as a baby. Wasn't that supposed to mess up kids? Maybe she was just like those hoppers on the corner out there. A tough life filled with bad decisions.

Or, it could have been the Honey Badgers. They certainly encouraged the bloodlust in her. Working for that barely sanctioned drug task force was where she learned how to kill and also where she realized how much she *liked* it. The Honey Badgers were like *21 Jump Street* and *Training Day* had spawned a nightmare baby. What if she hadn't joined? Maybe she'd be married with three kids and head of the PTA.

Stephanie chuckled at the thought.

Maybe the Honey Badgers had done her a favor.

She glanced to the left to keep tabs on the cop sitting in the corner of the bar.

Still nursing his beer.

She'd seen him before, but realized he posed no threat. He wore his badge, but he didn't *feel* like a cop. She never saw him do anything *coppy*. During her time in surveillance purgatory she'd seen a thug rough up a kid right outside the bar window. The cop hadn't moved. Hadn't even feigned interest.

Something's off with him.

Maybe he's lousy at being a cop. Lazy. Maybe when he was off duty, he was *off duty*. Though if he liked separation, spending his evenings sitting at the one bar with a clear view of the area's worst drug dealing corner seemed like a bad spot to hole up while wearing a cop badge.

"You want another?" asked the bartender.

Stephanie licked her lips, considering. Maybe it was time to pack it in for the evening. It seemed the drug trade was suffering a lull and—

"It's on me," said a voice to her left.

A man sat two stools down from Stephanie.

The cop.

"You don't look like you belong here," he added, smiling.

She surveyed the stranger. He was a handsome man for his age—maybe sixty something. He didn't look grizzled enough to be a cop who hung out in filthy dive bars during his down time.

"Neither do you."

The cop pulled his light jacket a little tighter, covering his badge. "I've seen you before."

The bartender put another iced tea in front of Stephanie and she cringed. The tea was terrible. She couldn't even imagine what a person could do to ice tea to make it taste that bad. She didn't like to drink during a hunt, but it occurred to her a glass of bourbon might be required to kill whatever was living in the tea.

The cop nodded toward her glass. "In the program?"

She laughed. "Right. Maybe I came to this nasty bar for the aesthetics. What better place to sober up?"

He shook his head. "No. I didn't think you came here not to drink. I think you came here to watch *them*." His eyes flicked in the direction of the dealers outside.

Stephanie frowned. "Do you have a point?"

Shaking his head, the cop stood to pull two dollars from his wallet. He put the money on the bar.

"I don't know what you're up to, but be careful."

Stephanie arched an eyebrow, amused. "Back at you."

The cop left and Stephanie watched him go, allowing her attention to drift to the men standing on the corner outside. *Men.* They were barely more than boys. She checked her watch. It was ten p.m. Last time their supplier had appeared at ten seventeen to gather cash and replace drugs. She needed to prepare to tail him.

Stephanie put a few more dollar bills on the counter.

"Thanks. I'll send you the bill for the stomach pump."

Eyes fixed on his newspaper, the bartender replied without missing a beat. "Try the shrimp cocktail next time if that's your thing."

Stephanie headed outside, walking briskly towards the junker car she'd rented for keeping a low profile in the neighborhood. Her long blonde hair tucked beneath a baseball cap, she'd worn baggy clothing to cover the rest of her impressive assets. She strode down the street affecting masculine gait so as not to shine like a beacon of weakness.

As she passed an alley, an arm hooked around her waist, jerking her into the shadows. Stephanie struck with the back of her fist, connecting with the attacker's windpipe. She heard him gasp. His arm slipped from her waist, but not before she saw a flash of movement to her left, too far away to be the same enemy. She felt the sharp crack of something striking her skull. From the pain, she guessed a ballpeen hammer.

The world spun and everything went black.

Her final thought was that her last meal had been that *revolting* ice tea.

CHAPTER THREE

Stephanie's head *throbbed*.

Her eyes fluttered open. Not that there was any point in seeing. She was certain she'd find herself in a dingy basement or dirt-floored warehouse. She'd been knocked on the noggin a few times in the past, and opening her eyes after a whack like that, she always found herself in a dreary—

French medallions.

The walls swarmed with French medallions. Small, dark blue patterns crawling floor to ceiling across a field of yellow. Not her favorite look, but somehow it worked with the solid navy draperies and the ivory settee pushed against the wall, opposite the bed.

The poster bed was grand. She would have been impressed by it if she weren't *tied to it.*

Stephanie jerked her arm and found it tightly secured by a thin nylon rope. If she could pull it up the post, away from the thicker base, it wouldn't be hard to snap the wood. She took a deep breath, tensing in preparation to yank her way to freedom.

"Please don't break my mother's bed."

Stephanie's head whipped to the left. The dark-haired

man standing beside her in khakis wore a light blue Burberry polo shirt, his sunglasses perched neatly on his head. He smiled, teeth gleaming from inside his chiseled jaw.

Oh my. Kidnappers had certainly grown more handsome since my time with the Honey Badgers.

The last man who'd kidnapped her had been a pudgy Nicaraguan wearing a torn Tom Petty t-shirt. He'd smelled like a wet dog.

This man... She sniffed. Was that *Creed Pure White* cologne?

Stephanie offered her captor her most endearing smile. "Do you always kidnap women and bring them to your mother's house?"

The man's eyes grew wide and he shook his head. "No, she'd kill—" He cleared his throat, gaze dropping to the floor. When he glanced back at her, it was as if he'd become a different person. He chuckled and pulled a dark, wooden chair from the corner to the side of the bed to sit.

"No. You must be special, baby. My name's Louis. It's a pleasure to make your acquaintance."

Stephanie had to bite her tongue to keep from laughing. This man, dressed like a prep school dreamboat, had suddenly adopted a voice that sounded like Scarface attempting to seduce a waitress.

I can't wait to see where this is going.

She held his gaze and smiled. "Do you think I'm special, Louis?"

The blood rose in his cheeks and he looked away.

"Ask her," said another voice.

Stephanie craned her neck to watch a tall, barrel-chested man enter the room. Spiky, red hair capped his olive-skinned face. If his coif had been dark hair dyed Ronald McDonald red, the result would have been strange enough. But this man had bleached his hair and then had it professionally colored to a strawberry blond. Against his swarthy skin, the effect was unsettling.

Louis turned, appearing annoyed by the intruder. "I am. I will—"

"Did you find someone else to work for? Someone besides Mateo?" asked the red-head, thrusting a chin in Stephanie's direction.

She felt her breath skip a beat. She hadn't heard Mateo's name from anywhere but the darkest recesses of her own brain in a very long time.

"Matay-who?" she asked, pretending not to recognize the name.

The man clucked his tongue. "My men saw you watching them a week ago. We took photos—"

"You mean *my* men," said Louis.

The tall man smiled like a snake ready to strike. "Right. You know that's what I meant, Louie. You the boss." He took a step forward and thrust out his hand so the two of them could run through the gestures of an elaborate handshake. Finished, Louis grinned and turned his attention back to Stephanie, as if to ensure she'd seen his mastery of the maneuver.

Oh you poor thing.

She could imagine him practicing the handshake in front of a mirror.

Louis jerked a thumb in the direction of the second man. "This is my main man, Pirro. He runs my crew."

Stephanie found it difficult to hide her embarrassment for Louis. She forced a smile and returned her attention to the strange redhead.

She found Pirro already staring at her. No little prep school boy hid behind *his* eyes. She recognized the empty anger of a man who had seen too much.

This could be a problem.

"Anyway, I bounced your picture off my uncle, girly. He

said you looked like a girl Mateo used to use. Said you were a killer."

Louis laughed. "Her? She's too pretty—"

Stephanie cut Louis short, her eyes never leaving Pirro. "Who's your uncle?"

"Diego Rodríguez."

Again Stephanie had to struggle to keep her pulse steady. She could picture Diego's face. He'd been a disloyal informant for the Honey Badgers. She'd thought he'd be dead by now. She took a deep breath.

"Never heard of him." She returned her attention to Louis and his expression belied his joy. She smiled and lowered her voice to a purr. "So, Louis...why don't you untie me and we can put all this behind us?"

Louis leered. "I can do that—"

"No," said Pirro.

Louis looked like a scolded child. Pirro's eyes widened, as if silently demanding his 'boss' follow a path on which they'd already agreed.

Louis sniffed. "I mean, I *could* let you go, but I won't. Not until you tell me why you're watching my men."

"I wasn't watching anyone."

Pirro sneered. "So you're just a big fan of the tea at the Shipwreck Bar?"

Stephanie smiled. "Tastes like grandma's."

Louis sighed. "If you're not the killer he told me you are, then I can't hire you."

Pirro rolled his eyes and walked to the opposite side of the room, clearly agitated. Louis wasn't following the script.

Stephanie took a deep breath and softened her demeanor once more. For whatever reason, Pirro, a true gangster and leader, needed to acquiesce to Louis, a boy playing gangster dress-up games.

Maybe playing the doe-eyed girl isn't the path to follow.

Maybe he wants me to be his gun moll.

"You want to hire me?" she asked Louis. "Who are you?"

She watched his chest puff with pride. "My name is Louis Beaumont."

"Beaumont? Any relation to Victor?"

Louis grinned. "He was my father."

From the other side of the room, Pirro grunted.

Ah.

The puzzle pieces were beginning to fit. Victor Beaumont had been the area's drug kingpin for decades. Following his death, his organization dissipated, but now here was his son, years later reclaiming the throne with the help of—

Stephanie glanced at Pirro. She could see he knew she'd figure it out. Pirro was from Columbia. True drug cartel royalty if his uncle was Diego Rodríguez. Pirro was using Louis' name to establish a foothold in Tampa.

Pirro had to be a good boy...for now.

She needed Louis on her side while Pirro was still allowing the pretender to give orders.

Time to make your fantasies come true, idiot.

"You need a lawyer?"

Louis laughed. "You're not a lawyer."

"Yes she is," mumbled Pirro.

"She is?"

Pirro nodded.

Louis looked at her, his brow crinkled with concern. "You're an assassin too though, right? You worked with his uncle in South America? You went by Ruby then. No...it was a Spanish word. *Rubia*?"

Stephanie felt the familiar flow of ice water in her veins. Order had been restored.

She *owned* Louis.

"Let's say for the sake of argument I'm this *Rubia*. What are you hoping I'll do for you?"

"I want you to kill my rival. If what Pirro tells me is right, that is what you do best."

"Your rival *what*? Drug dealer?"

Louis nodded. "I prefer the term *businessman*, but yes. You can kill his men, too if you have to. Pirro says you like killing. He says you're *crazy*, like that tall blonde chick in *Kill Bill*."

Louis looked like a kid staring at a Christmas package shaped like the bike he wanted more than anything in the world.

I can be his killer for a while. That takes care of both our problems.

She glanced at Pirro who stood leaning against the wall, glaring back at her.

I'll take care of Pirro later.

"What's killing drug dealers pay these days?"

Before Louis could speak, Pirro stepped forward.

"Don't you want to ask her why she was followin' us?"

Louis looked at Stephanie, who raised her eyebrows with expectation.

"I wasn't following you. I was following a cop who was following you," she said.

Louis looked at Pirro. "You have a cop following you?"

Pirro's expression darkened. "Yeah. We know about that guy. Why would she follow him?"

Stephanie sighed as if explaining her actions was the most tedious task she'd been asked to perform in some time.

"Because I was thinking of coming to Louis here and asking for a job. I figured spotting his enemies and letting him know about them would make me useful."

Louis clapped his hands together. "Great. You're hired."

Pirro thrust a hand in Stephanie's direction. "*Dude*, she didn't even know who you were a minute ago."

Stephanie laughed. "Are you kidding? He's Louis

Beaumont. Everyone knows him."

Louis beamed. "How about a million dollars?"

Pirro slapped his hand to his face and walked back to his place on the wall.

Stephanie pursed her lips and nodded to herself as if mulling the offer. She couldn't believe her luck.

"Make it a million two and I promise to take out anyone else around him who might consider revenge."

Louis yipped with excitement. "Deal."

"I told you I would get rid of that guy," said Pirro.

Louis frowned. "It's been like six months and nothing's changed. I need to hire a professional."

Stephanie nodded. "I'll get it done. I can't get much done with my hands tied to this bed though."

Louis motioned to the ties. Pirro pulled a switchblade from his pocket, glaring at Stephanie as he approached.

Easy there, little fella.

He cut the rope binding her to the bed posts. Feeling the bump on the back of her skull, she winced.

Pirro folded his knife and slipped it back into his pocket.

Louis helped her off the bed. "I owe you a *dinner*. Why don't we grab a bite and discuss the details?"

Stephanie stood. "You made one mistake."

Louis scowled. "What's that?"

"You didn't ask me to promise not to kill you when I'm done."

He laughed and put his arm around her shoulder. "I'm not worried. I have a lot of money. I think this is the beginning of a *beautiful* friendship."

CHAPTER FOUR

Present Day

Charlotte sipped lemonade on the porch of the tiki bar where Gloria Abernathy had asked to meet her. Gloria had once lived in Pineapple Port which, though a retirement community, was also where orphaned Charlotte grew up, raised by the local community after the death of her grandmother. She'd never dreamed the neighborhood would become her primary source of clients, but since becoming a private detective, it seemed that particular well of eccentricities would never run dry.

If Gloria hadn't left Pineapple Port, she could have been Charlotte's crown jewel. The woman had a penchant for petty revenge, and her confused victims would have kept any budding investigator's dance card full. With wide eyes, sharp features and a poof of auburn hair, Gloria looked more like a high-strung Pomeranian than a suburban avenger. But when wronged—real or imaginary—she attacked like a pit bull.

Charlotte lowered her lemonade. "You look good, Gloria."

The tiny woman touched her hair and grunted. "Lot of good it does me when my suitors go missing before I can try on the *suit*."

Charlotte cleared her thoughts and took another sip of lemonade. She'd learned long ago to avoid banter with retirees about their romantic lives. In her experience, the older people grew, the more often *modesty* lost a wrestling cage match to *honesty* and there would be no rematch planned. You never knew what you might *never* be able to unhear.

"So you're telling me this man was talking to you through his t-shirts?"

Gloria nodded. "He was. It was a very passionate relationship in its own way."

Charlotte chuckled. If the little woman could believe every move a stranger made was meant to annoy *her*, couldn't she also fancy a man's novelty tees were secret love messages?

"You're *sure* the messages on his shirts were meant for you?"

Gloria's mouth curved into a tight frown. "Why wouldn't you believe me?"

Charlotte thought for a moment. "I do. I believe you. It's just—I suppose if you thought he'd purposely cut you off in traffic I wouldn't be so sure—"

"What's that supposed to mean?"

"That temper of yours. Sometimes you believe people are out to slight you when they're just going about their lives."

Gloria looked away. "People can't just go about merrily ruining other people's lives. Running them off the sidewalk and whatnot."

Watching Gloria's taut jawline Charlotte realized two things. First, she'd better watch how she teased her potential client or she might find herself the focus of one of Gloria's revenge schemes. And second, Gloria's reference to sidewalk hogs seemed strangely specific.

Should I ask what she's done to those poor people? Maybe I should check missing persons...

"Don't be angry, Gloria. I just think sometimes you see

malice where there is none."

"Like when?"

"Well, I don't think the store manager who fired you for calling shoppers *fat* was out to ruin your life. I think he was out to avoid a lawsuit."

Gloria sniffed. "That's a matter of opinion. That kid was a porker. His mother should've been ashamed."

"That doesn't give you the right to put dead lizards in the store's fruit salad."

A strange smile rose to Gloria's lips. She leaned forward, her eyes somehow wide and squinty at the same time. Before that moment, Charlotte had only seen smiles like that on cartoon villains.

"You're right. I should have put the lizard in the *potato chips*. That kid wasn't going to eat a *fruit salad.* I could have killed two birds."

Feeling the heat radiating from Gloria's piercing stare, Charlotte leaned back in her seat. "Okay, okay. We're getting off track."

Gloria took a sip of her sweet tea and the vein bulging in her temple quelled like a subsiding flood. Once again she assumed the doe-eyed demeanor of a teacup poodle.

"Fine. So you *do* believe me?" she asked.

Charlotte released an involuntary sigh of relief. "I do. I'm just trying to get my facts straight. You and this man were sharing a moment every day. Winks, nods, hellos—and then he wrote words on his t- shirt?"

"Several words, in pen. All together, they said, *Hi, will you go out with me?* The question mark had its own shirt. It was in pink. Which was amazing, because I had chosen pink for *my* answer."

"Your answer? You made a shirt of your own?"

Gloria nodded so hard it looked like an invisible hand was dribbling her head like a basketball. "Yes. And *Yes* is what it said." She wrung her hands together, gaze darting toward the Gulf of Mexico, which lapped against brilliant white sands a hundred yards from where they sat. "Do you think I scared him away? Maybe he saw me coming with my big pink *Yes* and he got cold feet."

"It's possible. Not everyone can handle a woman with a big pink *Yes*."

Gloria nodded and then squinted at Charlotte, who quickly continued. "This man sounds pretty cheeky. He says *hello*, he touches your hand...he goes through all the trouble of writing words on his shirt... He doesn't sound like the kind of guy who would spook."

Gloria shook her head. "No. He radiated confidence. But in a white-knight sort of way. Not an arrogant way. Smiley Joe wouldn't be arrogant."

"Smiley Joe?"

"That's what I call him."

"Got it. And you haven't seen him since? Not at all?"

"No. The last day was the question mark and then nothing." Gloria's shoulders slumped. "I think he's been kidnapped."

"That seems unlikely. He might have just caught the flu."

"But it's been over a week—" Gloria paled. "Oh no. You think he *died* from the flu, don't you? If I find the person who gave him the flu—"

Charlotte laughed. "*No*, I'm not saying he died of the flu. I'm just saying he *could* have fallen ill or twisted an ankle or been called away on business. There are a lot of things that could have happened before we jump right to *kidnapped*."

Gloria put her napkin on the table. "Well, that's what you'll have to figure out."

"That's why I'm here."

A giant gold frog sat astride Gloria's middle finger, a pale green stone set in its center.

"That's quite a ring," said Charlotte.

Gloria glanced at it. "I'm into tree frogs. I couldn't resist it."

Charlotte wondered what animal she'd collect during her later years. Apparently, you had to pick one.

For now, she'd have to be happy with being an *officially hired* private detective.

A contented shiver ran down her spine.

Time to go and detect!

Feeling cool, she tilted her head back to capture the last drop of lemonade. The ice stuck to the bottom of the glass gave way and slid down to hit her in the nose. She righted the glass, and dabbed her wet face with a napkin as nonchalantly as possible.

I'm sure that happened to Sherlock Holmes all the time.

Charlotte stood. "Gloria, before I look into this for you, I need you to make me a promise."

"What's that?"

"If I find him, safe and sound, sitting on a porch somewhere with his wife, you have to promise me you won't do anything horrible to him."

Gloria's eyes bulged before she caught herself and cleared her countenance of all emotion. "Of course not."

Liar. But I won't call her on it. Better to live to fight another day...and earn a little money.

"Good." Charlotte put her napkin on the table. As she turned to leave, Gloria grabbed her hand.

"If he has a wife, you'll still tell me where he lives, right?"

CHAPTER FIVE

"I made you corn casserole."

Charlotte had barely stepped from the Volkswagen when Mariska thrust a bowl covered in painted roosters at her.

Charlotte cringed. She loved her adoptive mother's corn casserole, but the ingredients read like a magazine article entitled "Ten Things You Should Avoid if You're at Risk for Heart Disease."

When the Pineapple Port fifty-five plus community took her in after the death of her grandmother, someone should have warned her that accepting the offer meant a lifetime of sugary, fat-filled treats flying at her face like mosquitos at a summer picnic. Swat away the corn casserole and she'd be blindsided by a buy-one-get-one-free Whitman Sampler chocolate box.

"Every time you give me one of these casseroles I gain ten pounds." Charlotte heard a door slam and Mariska's best friend, Darla, appeared, chewing something as she approached. The woman's tongue stuffed the food to one side of her mouth to make room for talking. "You'll only gain nine pounds this time because I stole a spoonful or two."

Mariska lifted the lid on her dish. The surface of the

casserole looked as though a miniature pony had clomped across it, leaving spoon-sized divots in its wake.

Mariska scowled at Darla, who shrugged and attempted to pick a piece of corn from her teeth with her pinky nail.

Charlotte accepted the dish. "Thank you. And thank you for your car again. I swear I'm going to get one of my own soon."

Mariska smiled. "No problem. You can't keep my car but you *can* keep my dish."

Charlotte checked the bowl to be sure it was the one she thought it was. "Your rooster dish? I'd never dream of it."

Mariska's eyes filled with pity, as if Charlotte had been trapped on a desert isle and lost touch with the rest of the world. "I'm into *sea turtles* now."

"Oh, of course. Duh."

"How did your meeting go?" asked Darla.

"Good. Missing person, maybe. You'll never guess who hired me."

Mariska didn't let a moment pass. "The FBI?"

Charlotte's brow knit. "Why would the FBI hire me?"

"I don't know...that's who finds missing persons and you said *guess* so it seemed like a pretty good guess."

"Ah, well, no, not the FBI; I don't think I'm on their outsourcing radar yet. It was *Gloria*."

Darla's eyes grew wide. "Gloria who used to live here?"

"The same. Seems she was *this* close to meeting an eligible bachelor and he went missing."

"Went *running* is more like it," muttered Darla.

Charlotte chuckled. "I have to admit he does seem interesting. He was sending her messages written on his t-shirts."

Mariska and Darla's jaws both dropped as they said a single word in unison.

"Ryan."

Charlotte stared in wonder at their reaction. "You know him?"

"Ryan Flannigan. Right? Flannigan?" Mariska looked to Darla for confirmation.

Darla nodded. "Flannigan. Or O'Flanahan... something like that. He lived here years ago."

"How do you know it's him? Did he use the same trick to meet women here?"

Mariska nodded. "He was a piece of work."

Darla's expression mimicked Mariska's disapproval. "He caught it coming upstream and upgraded."

Charlotte's lip snarled. "You just made me imagine a naked old man swimming up a river to spawn."

Darla took a seat on the steps of Mariska's front door, collapsing to the cement with a grunt. "His unmarried son, Craig, died and all his money went to Ryan."

"So that's what you meant by upstream? He inherited his child's money instead of vice versa?"

Darla nodded.

Charlotte shook her head in wonder. "Someone needs to create an Urban Dictionary for retiree slang."

"His son Craig made a bunch of money in Silicone Valley," said Mariska.

Charlotte wanted to let Mariska's mispronunciation slide, but she heard the correction leap from her lips before she could stop it.

"Sili*con* Valley."

Mariska nodded. "Right. Where they make all the implants."

"Lot of money in implants," agreed Darla. "How many strippers do you think there are in the world?"

"And every one of them needs *two*," added Mariska.

Charlotte could feel the conversation slipping away from her. "No, it's Sili*con* Valley. That's where all the big Internet and software companies are in California. They don't make silicone breast implants there."

"Are you sure?"

Charlotte found herself wondering. "Now that you mention it...I don't know. I don't think they even make silicone implants anymore. But I know implants aren't what made Silicon Valley famous."

Mariska shrugged. Clearly, she disagreed.

Darla mumbled from her spot on the step. "Let's say there are five hundred thousand strippers, at two boobs each over twenty years..."

Charlotte decided to move on before she lost the ladies to complicated boob math. "How did Ryan's son die?"

"I don't remember. I just remember something was fishy about it," said Darla.

"Fishy as in Ryan had something to do with killing his own son?"

Both women shrugged.

"Okay. But we do know his son died, he inherited money and then moved to the beach, right?"

Darla nodded. "After bonking half the women in Pineapple Port."

"Not *me*," said Mariska.

Darla grew cross. "Well not me, either. You know who I mean."

Charlotte found her curiosity piqued. "Who?"

Darla shrugged. "Cathy. And Pris I think."

Mariska nodded.

Charlotte arched an eyebrow. "That's *two* people."

Darla and Mariska nodded in unison and Charlotte weighed the pros and cons of questioning the ladies' math again. "Two people aren't *half* of Pineapple Port."

Darla rocked back and forth in preparation to stand. "It's the *principle*."

Mariska agreed. "It's how he went about it."

"With confidence?"

Darla and Mariska both scoffed. "He was too good looking, that one," added Darla between grunts as she stood. "Him and his fancy cowlick—"

"Got it. Well, you've given me my first leads, anyway. I know his name is Ryan Flannigan or O'Flanahan—"

"Or Callahan," suggested Darla.

Charlotte grimaced. "So what you're really saying is it could be anything Irish."

Mariska nodded. "O'Callahan sounds right. He was from Boston."

Charlotte nodded. "Shocker. I'll check with Penny and see if she has records for where he moved. Thank you."

She crossed the street for home, pausing when she heard Mariska calling.

"Do you think you should warn Gloria about Ryan?"

Charlotte turned. "Don't you mean shouldn't we warn *him*?"

Darla and Mariska cackled.

CHAPTER SIX

"Whyja have to wear that shirt?"

Dallas took a step back and rubbed his knuckles.

Ryan Finnegan spat blood and peered down at his white tee, now splattered with red. Through the eye that hadn't swollen shut, he could see his shirt said, *Please?*

The message had been for a woman he passed walking on the Riverwalk every day. She'd probably never see it now. Worse, he'd never know her response to the question he'd so painstakingly asked her by writing a word per day on his chest.

Ryan lifted his head. "It's a long story." He tried to smile but the act made his face hurt. On the upside, his shoulders had gone numb. They'd tied his hands behind his back, causing his shoulders to burn. Now, if asked, he'd have to say his right cheek hurt more than any of his other body parts. Dallas was a lefty.

"It's just weird hittin' a dude with *Please?* on his chest. I already feel weird about you bein' so old." Out of breath, Dallas collapsed onto a chair opposite Ryan's.

Ryan guessed the boy was in his early twenties. Dallas looked like a lot of kids in Florida—impossibly thin, scruffy hair, drawers too big and held up by a thick belt, an apparent dentist phobia. Ryan called them "Espos" because they all looked like one of his son Craig's friends growing up. His name had been Espo.

Ryan's head swam. In his mind's eye he could see Craig and Espo playing soccer in his backyard.

What kind of name is Espo, anyway? I never thought about it. Nickname, probably. Short for Esposito?

"Hey, you hear me?"

Ryan snapped back to the present to find Dallas slapping his knee in an attempt to draw his attention back to the beating already in progress.

"What's that?" asked Ryan.

"I said, why don't you tell me what you've been doin' followin' our guys so I can quit beatin' on ya? You know this is just gonna get worse."

"I told you. I only talk to the big man."

Dallas sighed. "Sheeeet, Ryan. You're too old for me to be doin' this."

"Agreed."

"So why don't ya talk?"

"I told you, I only talk to—"

Dallas waved him silent. "Yeah, yeah." Dallas turned his head and snorted in a way that led Ryan to believe the boy had something seriously wrong with his sinuses. Dallas spat something and fished in his pocket for a cigarette.

"Those cigarettes are going to kill you."

Dallas grinned. "You're funny, tellin' me *I'm* gonna die. You're the one tied to a chair."

He put the cigarette in his mouth and lit it as Ryan eyed the tattoos on the boy's knuckles with his one good eye.

Dallas caught him staring. He stood, dropped the lighter back into the pocket of his baggy pants and held up his fists so Ryan could read the ink on the back of his knuckles. Each digit displayed a single letter, eight in total. The four letters on each hand created two words.

Ryan read the words aloud. "Your Dead."

Dallas nodded. "See? That's what I'm *sayin'*"

Ryan's brow knit, with some accompanying pain around his right eye socket. "What about my dead?"

"Your what?"

"Your knuckles are inquiring about *my* dead. If you're implying *I'm* about to be dead, it's Y-O-U apostrophe R-E, Dead. You need two more fingers on your right hand if you want to spell it right."

Dallas reversed his fists to read his knuckles, scowling before lowering his hands to his sides. "I *know*. It just didn't fit that way. I only got four fingers on each hand. If you don't count thumbs."

"Mm hm."

Dallas's eyes narrowed and he poked a finger in Ryan's direction. "You know if you don't talk soon, they're gonna bring in the *woman* to deal with you."

Ryan felt a cold chill run down his spine. He'd spent a lot of time making small talk with the boys on the corners over the last week. One of their favorite stories revolved around a female killer. Rumor had it their boss's business had recently tripled thanks to an assassin he'd brought in to wipe out the competition.

"The Rubia? She's real?"

Dallas nodded. "I think I saw her once."

Ryan recalled the most terrifying rumor he'd heard. A man had opened his front door to find a Christmas wreath made of human fingers hanging on his door, each arranged neatly, side by side in a circle. The rings on the fingers served both to identify the digits' owners and add a sparkly, festive air.

The woman had made the wreath with what was left of

the man's underbosses.

He had to ask. "What about the wreath?"

Dallas whistled. "Yep. I heard that one. Saw a photo, too. Freakin' crazy. That lady is no joke."

Ryan swallowed, the metallic taste of his own blood heavy on his tongue.

In hindsight, my plan may have been ill-advised.

He heard the sound of heels clicking in the hallway outside the room and the door opened. A blonde woman poked her head inside.

"Who's that?" she asked.

Ryan watched the boy pale. "The guy Louis wanted me to get for him."

The woman's gaze settled on Ryan.

She looked familiar. It was hard to tell through his swollen eye, but there was definitely something familiar about her. He'd seen her before.

He could tell who Dallas thought she was.

He couldn't be sure, but he thought he saw a flash of recognition ripple across her expression, and then The Rubia was   gone.

CHAPTER SEVEN

Charlotte held her dish of corn casserole high and away from Abby's flaring nose as she tucked it into her fridge. The soft-coated Wheaton terrier liked corn casserole as much as she did and precautions had to be made.

She knew she wasn't much better than the dog at restraint, and made a mental note to devise an eating plan—how much corn heaven she'd allow herself to devour per day.

Maybe I can draw a grid on the bowl with pretzel sticks and limit myself to one quadrant per day...

Mmm. Strips.

I could use bacon.

Grabbing Abby's leash from the hook by the door, Charlotte took the dog for a bathroom break in order to put some distance between herself and the casserole. While planning forced moderation, she'd managed to mentally add *bacon* to the cholesterol nightmare already taunting her. Time to run away before she dropped her face into the bowl like it was a feedbag.

It was late November and a cool seventy-five degrees—nice temperature in which to walk the dog and not have to wring sweat from her clothes upon her return. Even Abby appeared to have an extra spring in her step.

A few streets down from her own, Charlotte heard shouting and spotted a man arguing with a woman in front of a recently vacated home. It didn't take long to identify the arguers. Penny, Pineapple Port's owner, raised her bony arm in the air to punctuate a point. Penny's long-suffering community foreman, Roberto, raised his hands in response, marching toward his truck, reeling off his own complaints in Spanish. Hopping in the community's maintenance truck, he slammed the door and drove off with a screech of tires.

"You'll never work here again!" Penny shrieked after him.

"Trouble?"

Penny turned, her hand on her chest.

"Charlotte! Why would you sneak up on me like that? You could have scared me to death."

"I didn't sneak up on you. You just didn't hear me with all the screaming going on."

Penny motioned to a second truck parked in the driveway. "Lazy man. He filled the truck for me and then refused to drive it to the pawn shop."

Charlotte perked. "Declan's pawn shop?"

"Hock o'Bell."

"Right. That's Declan's."

"Whatever."

Charlotte scowled. "*Declan.* My *boyfriend.* You've met him like a dozen times."

Penny waved the comment away with the flick of a skeletal wrist. "I can't drive this truck. It's too big."

Charlotte eyed the open-bed pickup. It was smaller than Penny's SUV, but she knew that argument would get her nowhere. "Why didn't you have Declan come pick it up?"

"He wanted to charge me a hundred dollars."

"How much did Roberto charge you?"

"Charge me? *Nothing.* He works for me." She scoffed and

stared in the direction Roberto had sped. "*Used* to work for me."

If her beady eyes had lasers, Roberto's truck would have exploded.

Charlotte tried not to laugh. Penny threatened to fire Roberto on a daily basis. She was about to offer her goodbyes and continue her walk when the *amount* of furniture in the bed of the second truck still sitting in the driveway drew her attention.

"Did you say Roberto moved all that?"

Penny nodded. "It took him *forever*."

"By himself?"

"I was here to supervise. Up until he said he had to have *lunch*." She waggled her index and middle fingers like twitchy bunny ears to enact air quotes around the word *lunch*, as if an afternoon meal was a concept Roberto had made up to annoy her.

"Right. Tell you what..." Charlotte slowed, worried she was about to make a mistake. She understood Penny would take advantage of any kindness offered, but she also knew asking for a favor would be easier if Penny felt as if she'd won something in the deal.

"I'll drive it to Declan's."

Penny hoisted an eyebrow. "That's lovely, but I need it taken to the Hock o'Bell."

"That *is* Declan's."

"Hm. If you say so."

Penny turned to leave and Charlotte reached out to touch her arm. It reminded her of handling a turkey wing on Thanksgiving.

"Wait, I need some information from you first."

Penny felt the pocket of her shorts. "Right. I have the address of the pawn shop written down here somewhere—"

"I know the address."

"Are you sure?"

Charlotte took a deep breath. "*Declan is my boyfriend.*"

Penny sniffed. "I hope the owner of that shop pays your boyfriend well. Charging people a hundred dollars to pick up a few things—"

"A few things? That truck looks like a pioneer family of ten is about to make its way West. And the owner *is* my boyfriend. Declan is the owner..." Charlotte sighed, disappointed in herself for trying. "You know what? Never mind."

Penny didn't seem to hear. "It's mostly junk. Man who lived here had no taste at all. No one buys that stuff anymore, but he left it behind like a lazy bones and I figured I deserve to make a few dollars off it."

Charlotte squinted one eye. "Left it behind? Didn't the man who lived there *die*?"

Penny scrubbed the roof of her orbital cavities with her eyes, back and forth, until Charlotte worried the irises would never drop back into place again. She was like a broken slot machine, caught between symbols. "Death doesn't mean you can just leave your crappy furniture all over the place. He could at least have the courtesy to have responsible family to clean out his hovel."

"Should you be calling the houses you built hovels?"

Penny ignored the question and continued. "I got lucky though. That pawn store fellow is paying me too much for this trash. *Idiot.*"

Charlotte rubbed the bridge of her nose in an attempt to calm herself. She'd almost forgotten the point of this painful interaction was to plumb Penny for information.

Time to refocus.

"I need to know about a man who used to live here."

"You already said it. *He died.* Fell over dead at the bowling alley. Thank goodness he wasn't in our weight room or—"

"Not the man who rented this house. I'm looking for someone who used to live in Pineapple Port maybe six or seven years ago. He'd be in his early sixties now. Handsome, from what I've been told. Bit of a ladies' man. Ryan Flannigan? Or Callahan—"

"Finnegan."

"You remember him?"

"Certainly. I remember everything."

Charlotte grimaced. *Right. Except who Declan is.*

"Do you know where Mr. Finnegan moved?"

Penny nodded. "That big tower out on the beach. The white one that looks like a cheap wedding cake."

"Do you remember the address? His apartment number?"

"No. We're not pen pals or anything. I remember the building though because I'd tried to get George to buy us a place there when they first built them and he wouldn't have it. Worth four times as much now. We could have made a killing. That man never listens to me."

"But you're sure that's where he moved?"

"Absolutely."

"Great. Okay. I'm going to take Abby home and then I'll come back and take the truck to Declan."

"I need you to take it to the pawn shop."

"Right. My bad."

"Wonderful. Thank you." Penny turned and held up a hand to wave goodbye. "Don't forget to pack up the stuff on the porch."

Charlotte's attention snapped to the porch where she could see more knick-knacks piled high.

"Wait, what?"

"Thank you!" Penny called over her shoulder and turned the corner without another sound.

CHAPTER EIGHT

The bell in Declan's shop rang as Charlotte entered.

"I have a truck of stuff from Penny out here," she announced, wiping her brow. Sweat of shame glistened on her forearm. Packing the rest of Penny's junk into the truck had taken nearly an hour. Once again she'd allowed Penny to abuse her naturally helpful nature.

Fool me once, shame on you, fool me a hundred and eighty thousand times...

Declan's employee, Blade, turned and grinned at her from beneath his impressive, droopy mustache. Blade was an enormous man with a shadowy history and a penchant for wearing shirts featuring one kind of weapon or another. Though he appeared menacing, he was a teddy bear of a giant and the best salesman Declan had ever hired, much to Declan's chagrin.

"Let me help you with that, Miss Charlotte," said Blade, lumbering toward the door.

"I appreciate it."

Declan appeared from the back office, eyes widening when he spotted her. "Hey, what are you doing here?"

Charlotte smiled. "I missed you, too."

He gave her a peck on the cheek. "I didn't mean it like that. I wasn't expecting you."

"I know. Penny duped me into bringing you a truck full of furniture."

Declan eyed her haul through the front windows. "Oh, right. I'm going to make a killing on that stuff. I tried to tell Penny she wasn't asking enough for it, but she was so determined to get her price I had to give it to her."

Charlotte chuckled. That Penny wasn't getting the deal she *thought* she was made her feel warm and fuzzy inside.

"Do you want to go to the beach? I need to see if someone lives out there and we can use it as an excuse to sit on the sand for a bit."

"Is this for a job?"

She nodded, finding it hard to squelch her joy at being employed as an *official* private detective. "Possible missing person. Probably nothing but I need to go check his last known residence."

"You sound so official."

"I know. Don't I?"

"You want to go now?"

"Now would be good if you can swing it."

He nodded. "I can leave Blade in charge."

Blade pushed open the front door with his behind, toting a large table held pressed against his chest. The furniture seemed too large for a human to carry, but Blade carted it in and flipped it to its feet like it was made of Styrofoam.

Declan stared. "Blade, I'm going to go out for a few hours if you could hold down the fort?"

"Fort?"

"The *store*. Watch the store."

Blade nodded. "Understood. But I wouldn't call this place a *fort*. Multiple sources of entry. Hard to seal and defend. The glass in the front alone..."

Blade trailed off, shaking his head grimly as he surveyed the windows. Charlotte found herself staring at glass, imagining a horde of zombies spilling through like sewer rats.

Declan opened his mouth and then shut it again. He turned his attention to Charlotte. "Ready. Do you have what you need for the beach?"

Charlotte nodded. "Yep, brought it with me. We can swing by your place on the way so you can grab some trunks."

They bade farewell to Blade and took Declan's car to his home, not far from Pineapple Port. His Uncle Seamus stood outside, talking loudly on the phone.

"No. No, it's gonna be rosy. You'll be *fine.* I'll be there in a bit. Right. Bye." Seamus dropped the phone from his ear as they approached. "Hail, young lovers. What are you up to on this fine morn?"

Declan's gaze dropped to Seamus's boxer shorts—the only stitch of clothing the man wore. "It's almost noon, Seamus. Did you just wake up?"

"Maybe."

"Didn't we talk about you roaming around in front of my neighbors in your boxers?"

Seamus scratched his beard and winked at Charlotte, clearly amused to be scolded by his nephew. "Maybe."

Seamus had been crashing at Declan's for months since returning from Miami, where he'd served as some sort of cops' snitch. She wasn't sure about the details—nothing Seamus said was ever completely the truth anyway—but he'd helped her earn her detective's license and was always in a charming mood, so she let slide his embellishments and omissions.

Charlotte scowled at Seamus's bloodshot eyes. "Everything okay? You look a little rough."

Seamus shrugged. "That was Jackie on the horn. She thinks someone is messing with her club."

"What club?"

"Her underground disco for geezers—*Slipped Disc'o*."

Charlotte laughed. "*Jackie* owns that secret old people club? I've heard rumors about one around the Port but I never dreamed *Jackie* owned it."

"Some detective you are," said Declan.

"Very funny."

Seamus grinned. "Quite a perk for your girlfriend to have her own bar, eh?"

Charlotte suddenly felt a little wounded. "Why did she keep it a secret from *me*?"

"She's tried to keep it a secret from the Pineapple Port crew. Doesn't want her neighbors looking down on her—what with her husband and all."

"Why would people look—" Charlotte stopped, realizing there were plenty of Pineapple Port residents who'd think it improper for Jackie to own a disco. The fact that Jackie's deceased husband had been a notorious slum lord didn't help. Keeping her disco a secret from the neighbors also saved her from having customers so close to home. They'd be clucking their tongues about the disco on Monday and hitting her up for coupons on Friday.

Jackie was a smart lady.

Charlotte waved away the rest of her sentence. "Never mind. I totally get it. What do you mean she thinks someone is *messing* with her?"

"Some wanker left a dead skunk on her doorstep about the same time some guys showed up asking to buy the place. She thinks someone is trying to muscle her into sellin'."

"Oh no. What do you think?"

Seamus shrugged. "She's got a bouncer the size of an oak tree, but he's got the flu. That's why I look like the devil. I was up all night playin' bouncer. That was her on the phone telling me two more men stopped by and made her an offer."

"And she doesn't want to sell?"

"No. The whole affair has made her jumpy. I promised I'd go back out and see her." He squinted at his nephew. "How'd you like a little bouncer work tonight?"

Declan grimaced. "You think you need help?"

Seamus shrugged again and sucked on his tooth with his tongue until the suction gave way with a snap.

Declan spent another moment awaiting a definitive answer and then gave in. "Sure. I'll swing by when we get back."

Seamus grinned and slapped his nephew on the shoulder as Declan headed inside to change.

Charlotte crossed her arms against her chest and prepared to make small talk with a middle-aged man in his boxers for a few minutes.

"Did Jackie tell Frank about these threats?"

Seamus tilted his head forward and peered from beneath his brow. "Nah. Sheriff Frank doesn't know about the club. Let's keep it that way for now."

Charlotte nodded. *Duh.* If the rumors she'd heard were true, Jackie's disco wasn't exactly legal. She'd heard this mysterious club referred to as an underground dance hall for the fifty-five and over crowd, complete with illegal poker games in the back. Sheriff Frank was a good guy and Darla's husband, but he did like to play things by the book. Best to keep him in the dark as long as possible.

"Does Jackie know who these men are?"

"Call themselves *businessmen* but from her description they sound more like thugs. I haven't laid eyes on them yet. Probably want to turn the place into a teenage drug den or sometin'. I'll take care of it, but I'd like your man's help if you don't mind."

In truth, Charlotte didn't love the idea of Declan putting himself in danger, but she knew he wouldn't stand by and leave everything to his aging uncle.

"I'm sure he's happy to help. I'll come too. Maybe I can uncover something about who's bullying her."

Seamus grinned "Two private dicks and some muscle. We'll take care of this in no time."

"Please don't call me a private dick."

"Sorry, true, I'm more of a *public* dick myself."

Charlotte snorted a laugh.

Declan reappeared in walking shorts and a polo shirt that spilled neatly from the tops of his impressive pecs. He swam every day in a lap pool behind his home and while Charlotte wasn't sure why he worked out so hard, she wasn't complaining.

"I ditched the trunks. I imagine we'll be skipping the beach in order to get to Jackie's?"

Charlotte smiled. "You know me so well. Maybe we'll grab some lunch though."

Declan slapped his uncle on the back. "Later old man."

Seamus winced and scowled. "I'll old man *you*."

Declan and Charlotte drove to the beach and parked on the street outside Ryan Finnegan's condo. Round and white, Charlotte had to agree his building did conform to Penny's idea of a "wedding cake." There didn't seem to be anything *cheap* about it though—it had a manned gate blocking their entry to the parking lot.

They exited the car and Charlotte stood with her hands on her hips, chewing on her lip as she stared at the guard gate. She glanced at Declan and his shoulders slumped a little.

"Let me guess, you want me to distract the guard while you slip inside."

She smiled. "It's almost scary how well you know me now."

"Scary's the word for it, alright."

She gave him a quick kiss on the cheek. "I'll buy lunch."

He sighed. "Deal."

Declan approached the gate and struck up a conversation with the woman inside the booth while Charlotte slipped by and jogged to the front door of the building. She tugged on the handle.

Locked.

A moment before she could start hitting random intercom buttons hoping to find someone who would buzz her in, a man left the lobby. She grabbed the door and smiled as he passed, to appear as though he'd saved her time spent fishing for her key. He nodded and continued on his way.

She entered the 90s Tuscan-styled lobby and wandered to a small, unattended mail room in the back. Slipping inside, she found a roster of tenants and trained down the list until she spotted Ryan's name and apartment number.

Bingo.

Charlotte took the elevator to the sixth floor and followed the signs to condo six hundred and one.

The stark white door of Ryan's condo featured none of the decorations displayed by some of his neighbors. No brass eagle knocker, no shell wreath, no flip-flop door mat.

She knocked.

No answer. A window in the thick cement wall beside the door had the blinds open, so she stood on her toes and peered inside.

Even from her limited view, she could tell Ryan's main living area hadn't been tidied in a while. Two of the dining room chairs lay on their sides. On the table, a glass had spilled, bleeding what looked like a pool of orange juice across the table top. Plate shards scattered across a faux wood tile floor.

Not good.

That's what we in the business like to call "signs of a struggle."

She didn't have to be a detective to know *signs of a*

struggle didn't bode well for Ryan.

Charlotte retrieved her phone from her pocket and called Sheriff Frank. His voice barked into the line.

"Frank here."

Charlotte grimaced. She wasn't sure why she *ever* thought she'd catch Frank in a cheery mood. "You sound agitated."

"Aaah, some yahoo took a dump in a hotel pool and now he's running around with his shorts in his hand, waving them around like a victory flag."

"Alcohol involved?"

"Boy, you really are a detective now, aren't you?"

She giggled. "Well, I hate to bother you when you're in the middle of serious police business, but I need a favor."

"Great. Hit me. Anything to keep from watching this ding dong bounce around this pool."

"Literally."

Frank grunted and Charlotte continued.

"Remember Gloria Abernathy? She moved from the neighborhood a few months ago?"

"Little lady. Sort of permanently shocked in the eye department?"

"Right. She hired me to find a man she thought went missing. I'm at his apartment now, and there are clear signs of a struggle."

"Let me guess, you pulled a *Darla* getting in there?"

Charlotte smirked. Frank's wife Darla had taught her how to pick locks. She'd even gifted her with her first lock-picking kit. Seems Darla had spent some time with some questionable people before marrying the local heat.

Charlotte felt relieved she didn't need to lie to Frank about how she'd come upon her information. For once.

"No, I restrained myself. Just peeked through a window. But that's why I'm calling you. He's not answering the door and, as far as I know, he could be in there unconscious on the floor or something. I hate to get the police over here for nothing...could be he just had a wild party and is passed out on his bed."

"I'll swing by. What's the address?"

"That's the other thing, I'm out of your jurisdiction. I'm at the beach."

"So... Did you call me to ask for my permission to pick his lock?"

"Pretty much. And to see if you had any words of wisdom before I check things out."

"And if I say *no*, are you going to do it anyway?"

"Yes. But I'll feel better about it with your blessing. Should I be swept into anything dicey, you can honestly state I *discovered* the scene and didn't *cause* it."

"I *don't* know that. And you think I'll take the stand and tell a judge I *told* you to pick a man's lock?"

"Good point."

Frank sniffed. "Right. Well, I guess we're through here then."

"Great. No words of wisdom?

"Not anything you don't already know. Don't touch anything. Don't get yourself killed."

"Ooh, that's a good one. I'll write that one down..."

Frank hung up, but she thought she heard him chuckle before going.

Charlotte put her phone back in her pocket and pulled out her lock picks. The lock was old and gave way immediately. She pushed open the door.

"Hello?"

Nothing.

She tiptoed past the mess and poked her head into the bedroom. The bed was neatly made. The view of the gulf from the balcony was gorgeous. On the sofa table sat a photograph of a young man smiling. His pose smacked of some sort of corporate headshot. She guessed that was Craig, Ryan's deceased son.

If it wasn't, Gloria was really barking up the wrong tree.

But for the mess at the table, everything seemed to be where it should be, though the décor confirmed the apartment as a bachelor's. Black leather sofa. Enormous television.

No sign of Ryan Finnegan.

She took a moment to study the mess in the dining room. The thin layer of orange juice had dried into a shiny, sticky armor, though some of the liquid in the glass was still just that. Liquid. The broken shards of plate on the ground had dried egg stuck to it. She guessed that the mess had been that way for a few days.

Charlotte hadn't found Ryan dead. That was a step in the right direction. But she hadn't found any sign that he'd left peacefully either.

She exited and locked the door behind her.

Outside, she walked past the gate with no particular concern. Condo gatekeepers didn't care who *left*.

She found Declan waiting for her next to his car.

"How'd it go?" she asked.

He shrugged. "Sasha there in the booth says it's going to rain later today, she saw a Maserati earlier which she someday hopes to own, and her brother washes cars, *like for reals*. I have his card."

"Excellent. I'll be sure to call the next time I need my Maserati waxed."

"Did you find who you're looking for?"

She shook her head. "It looks like he left in a real hurry and someone might have helped him along."

"Was there blood?"

She laughed. "You're so dramatic. You know not

everything I investigate involves blood."

"No blood? Yeesh. You can bore me with the details at lunch."

Her gaze drifted across the street to an open-air restaurant called *Shark Town Tiki Bar*. The establishment was dark and dingy and, but for the name, didn't deserve to be so close to the ocean.

"Let's eat over there."

Declan cocked an eyebrow. "Really?" He paused and Charlotte watched as his surprised expression morphed into one of suspicion. "Ah. You have a hunch your guy spent some time there."

"I do. It's at his doorstep."

He nodded. "Makes sense."

They crossed the street and entered the bar. The yellowing polyurethane bar top trapped a sea of shells and beer caps beneath it, like a beach-bum dinosaur's DNA sealed in amber. Charlotte sat and lifted her hands in the air as the sticky surfaces threatened to permanently claim her flesh. At the opposite end of the long bar, an older woman with a platinum helmet of hair sat drinking a pink cocktail. The bartender, a pudgy man in his mid-forties wearing a parrot-patterned short sleeve shirt, approached without smiling.

"What can I getcha?"

Charlotte forced a smile as her gaze swept over a row of cheesy, beach-and-bikini-based advertisements behind the bar. "Corona light?"

The bartender nodded to Declan, who wore the same unconvincing smile Charlotte imagined she'd projected.

"Same."

With a nod, the bartender walked in the direction of the platinum blonde to grab the beers.

Charlotte leaned toward Declan and whispered. "You order a bottled beer because you're afraid to use the glasses in this joint?"

He answered without changing his expression. "Yep. You?"

"Yep. Want to order some sushi?"

He laughed.

The bartender returned with two Coronas and Charlotte spoke before he could lumber away.

"We were looking for my uncle and thought he might be here. Ryan Finnegan. Do you know him?"

The blonde woman's head swiveled. "Ryan's your uncle?"

Charlotte nodded. "You know him?"

The woman flicked out a crimson tipped index finger like a switch blade and poked it in Charlotte's direction. "You tell that bastard where to go for me."

Charlotte heard Declan mumble, "Oh boy," behind her.

"Do you know where my uncle is? He was supposed to be here but we knocked on his door and he didn't answer."

The woman scowled so tightly it was as if all her features had scurried into the center of her face. "He was supposed to meet me, too. Maybe I shouldn't be so offended seeing as he stood up his own niece." She laughed bitterly to herself.

"He was supposed to meet you today?"

"A week ago."

Charlotte had the passing thought that the woman *looked* like she'd been sitting there waiting for a week.

"When was the last time you saw him?"

The woman rolled her eyes. "The last time I saw him he was sneaking around my bedroom picking his clothes up off the floor, thinking I was asleep."

"About a week ago?"

"Yeah. He forgot his phone. I told Pete to tell him I'd meet him here to give it to him. I couldn't call him 'cuz—"

"You had his phone. Who's Pete?"

She nodded toward the bartender.

"I'm Pete," he said, digging in his ear with his middle finger.

"This is where we hooked up, so I thought Pete could relay the message." The woman said *relay the message* as if she were translating a fancy foreign phrase.

Charlotte turned to the bartender. "You know Ryan?"

He shrugged. "He comes in a couple times a week for a rum and Coke. I don't know him other than he hates flat Coke. Got a real stick up his butt about flat Coke."

Charlotte nodded. Fascinating factoid, but she doubted Ryan's distaste for flat Coke would blow the case wide open.

"So, neither of you have seen him for a week?"

Pete nodded. "'Bout that. I told him Sally had his phone. He told me to tell her he'd meet her here."

"And he never showed."

Sally leaned down to grab her purse, nearly toppling from her bar stool as she stooped. She aborted the mission and took a moment to steady herself, before fishing for the large bag's handles with her sandal-clad foot. She hooked the straps with her toes and lifted the bag high enough off the ground to grab it. Probing inside, she produced a cell phone and slid it down the bar toward Charlotte. It went wildly left, but Pete caught it.

"There's his stinkin' phone. If you see him, tell him we're *through*."

Pete handed Charlotte the phone and she pushed a few buttons.

"What kind of phone is that?" asked Declan, peering over her shoulder.

"Old. Very old. And very dead."

"Where are you going to find a charger? Do you need to go back to his apartment?"

Charlotte chuckled. "Pineapple Port is a retirement community. If I can't find a charger for this there, it doesn't exist."

CHAPTER NINE

Mariska pulled open her kitchen drawer, revealing a sea of black phone charger cords. A few had plugs large enough to serve as doorstops.

"One of these should work," said Mariska.

Charlotte tried four before she found a strange gap-toothed prong that fit Ryan's phone perfectly. "That'll do it. I knew as soon as I saw his phone you'd have something that worked."

"It isn't the same as mine."

"No, but it was personally signed by Alexander Graham Bell so I knew I had a shot." Charlotte glanced at Mariska's own ancient flip-phone and Mariska tucked it to her chest protectively.

"My phone works *fine*."

"When I send you photos they show up as Chinese characters. That's not how that's supposed to work."

Mariska grunted. "Want some sausages and peppers? Declan, have you had my sausages and peppers?"

Declan looked up from where he sat beside Charlotte. "I have. And I'd love to, but we need to get to Jackie's club—"

Charlotte's elbow jerked against Declan's ribs and he

stopped short with a tiny *oof.*

Mariska's brow wrinkled. "Did you say Jackie's *club*?"

"Uh, hm? I think I left my car running. Just a second..." Declan grabbed his keys from the counter, flashed Mariska a smile and dashed from the house.

Mariska watched him go and then focused her curiosity on Charlotte. "Did he say Jackie's *club*? What does that mean?"

Charlotte sighed. "You know I can't tell you or you'll tell everyone."

"I will not."

"You told me what I was getting for Christmas every year, *days* before I could open my presents."

"You wanted to know."

"Of course I *wanted* to know, but you're supposed to *not tell me.*"

"I didn't let you have them until Christmas."

"I got my ten-speed bike on Thanksgiving."

Mariska huffed. "That doesn't count. It was too big to keep hidden. You were a very inquisitive little girl."

Charlotte sighed. "Fine. I'll tell you, but only because if I don't you'll go around asking about Jackie's mysterious club until everyone in Pineapple Port is trying to figure out what you're talking about."

Mariska's expression didn't change, so she continued.

"Jackie has a secret dance club."

Mariska's eyes grew wide. "At her house?"

"No, out in the woods thirty minutes or so from here. It's a disco for older people."

"Why didn't she ever tell me?"

"She didn't want anyone in Pineapple Port to know. Remember, her husband was a slum lord—she doesn't want her neighbors thinking *she's* shady, too. Plus neighbors are a pain."

"What's that supposed to mean?"

Charlotte sighed. "You know. It's a *bar.* There's always complications when alcohol is involved. She didn't want her neighbors to get into fights and end up mad at *her.* I imagine she didn't want you all plying her for free drinks, either."

Mariska's chest puffed. "I would *never* expect free drinks."

"Mm hm. Anyway, she's apparently having a little trouble and she asked Seamus for help, who in turn asked Declan."

"And you're going, too? What kind of trouble?"

Charlotte nodded. "Nothing big. Silly stuff."

Mariska frowned. "Well, you be careful. Those dance clubs are full of drugs."

"You think if I go there they're just going to pelt me with drugs?"

"You never know."

Charlotte checked Ryan's phone. The ancient piece of equipment wasn't a speedy charger. She unplugged it from the wall.

"Do you mind if I take this plug?"

"No."

"Thanks." Charlotte gathered up the cord and headed for the door.

"Keep an eye on your cocktail if you drink at the club. Don't drink any rooskies," Mariska called after her.

Charlotte paused. "It's *rufies*, and this is exactly what Jackie was afraid of. I'm sure the club isn't scary. It's a disco for *old people*."

"Oh."

Charlotte barely had the time to put her hand on the knob to leave before Mariska called out again.

"Stay away from the dirty old men!"

CHAPTER TEN

Mariska crawled onto her bed to peer out the window facing the street. She heard the toilet flush and her husband, Bob, stepped out of the bathroom.

"Did I hear Charlotte?" he asked.

Mariska nodded and watched as Declan and Charlotte pulled from her driveway and drove away.

"What are you doing?"

Mariska crawled backwards off the bed. "Nothing."

Bob turned and strolled from the bedroom, muttering under his breath. "I swear you get weirder every day."

Mariska opened her flip phone and dialed Darla.

"Hello?"

"Darla, Jackie has a bar dance club disco."

"What?"

Mariska cast a furtive glance down the hall. She made a little cave with her hand over her mouth and the phone to be sure Bob couldn't overhear.

"Jackie has a bar dance club disco," she whispered.

"What's a bar dance club disco? And why are you whispering?"

Mariska heard the familiar creak of the front door. Bob

had wandered outside to do his afternoon chores. Creeping deep into the living room, farthest away from the garage where most of the afternoon chores occurred, Mariska lowered in her comfy Laz-E-Boy.

"Charlotte told me Jackie owns some sort of dance club disco with a bar out in the forest."

"You mean a booze bar? That kind of bar? Out in what forest?"

"I don't know. She said it's out in the woods."

"You mean out in the *swamp*." Darla fell silent and then continued, sounding more irritated than she had a moment before. "Why wouldn't Jackie tell us she had a booze bar in the swamp? That sounds like a hoot."

"Charlotte thinks she doesn't want us to think poorly of her."

Darla snorted. "I think poorly of her because she *didn't* tell me she had a booze bar. I could have saved a fortune on drinks."

Mariska pursed her lips, realizing Charlotte might have had a point about neighbors expecting discounts.

"When is it open?" asked Darla.

"I don't know. Charlotte and Declan are on their way over there now. Jackie needed something and they're helping Seamus do whatever it is."

"Hm. We should go there."

"But they'd see us."

"That's the point. We'll confront Jackie for keeping her secret."

"Confront her?"

"Not mean-like. We'll just go when we know she's there, so she can't pretend it isn't there, because we *know* it's there and there are witnesses."

Mariska considered Darla's logic. "And it's daylight now so it might be easier to find..."

"Good point. We don't want to end up hip-deep in alligators."

"I thought the pythons ate all the alligators."

"I think it depends on the day of the week."

Mariska sprang to her feet and then sat again, realizing she still didn't know where the club was. "Tell you what...I'll pick you up in fifteen minutes. I need time to find out where the club is exactly. What should we wear? Should we wear dance clothes?"

Darla laughed. "Dance clothes? Like what? A tutu?"

"No, I was thinking maybe I should wear something nicer than shorts though."

"Hmm. I see what you're saying. She might have afternoon dancing."

"I wonder how we can find out what to wear."

"We'd know if she *invited* us."

"Exactly. I think we should wear something a little warmer because she probably has the air conditioning up so the dancers don't get sweaty."

"That's a good point."

"Okay, I'll see you soon."

Mariska disconnected and scurried to the bedroom to put on her stretchy slacks. They looked nice and she could move in them, just in case she had to dance. She swapped her every day scoop-neck tee for a matching flowing black-and-white blouse, and, feeling too staid, added a chunky bright lime necklace. Slipping into shiny black flats, she opened her underwear draw and felt beneath her bras. Her fingers touched plastic and she retrieved the object she'd hidden there.

Her smartphone.

Day to day she still used her flip phone—still suffered Charlotte's ribbing for owning such an archaic piece of technology—because she didn't want Charlotte to know she'd bought a smart phone.

More specifically, she didn't want Charlotte to know *why* she'd bought a smart phone.

The fancy phone sprang to life and Mariska clicked on the locator app.

She'd bought it, because smart phones could track your loved ones.

Mariska smiled as the glowing dot representing Charlotte appeared on her screen.

It had taken Mariska two tries, fiddling with Charlotte's phone when she wasn't looking, but she'd managed to connect the two phones.

She could find Charlotte anywhere.

If that girl thinks she's going to become a private detective without someone keeping an eye on her, she has another thing coming.

Mariska touched up her makeup, grabbed her purse and headed outside.

Bob sat on the cement fiddling with the golf cart battery. He looked up at her as she opened her car door.

"Where you going all gussied up?"

"Darla and I are going shopping."

He rolled his eyes as she slid into her Volkswagen and waved at him through the window.

CHAPTER ELEVEN

It was time to quit.

Stephanie couldn't live with her own hypocrisy anymore. She'd made a little progress. She'd been determined to turn over a new leaf of sorts, but she couldn't kid herself any longer. Momma's serial killer DNA was having too much fun working for Louis. Killing bad people for a bad person wasn't putting the "heal" in double-helix any time soon.

She had to stop.

Declan wouldn't consider her current occupation in the gray area as a *win*. She wished she could stop thinking about him. She'd realized too late there was something about that tall, dark handsome man—their history, the way he knew her—she *needed* him. He kept her stable.

He'd always been her favorite pet. Pets weren't supposed to *stray*. Like a good dog, he was noble. One only had to meet his do-gooder, wannabe detective girlfriend to know he was attracted to the light. Once he'd run around the jungles of Columbia battling drug cartels with her—now he preferred loping around with Princess Sunshine and the Golden Girls.

Sad. I need to save him from himself.

She'd thought working for Louis culling a rival drug crew

could make her rich *and* satiate her bloodlust. No one could hold it against her for killing drug dealers, right? She was a *white hat*, now.

But what had started as a tiny itch at the back of her brain was becoming impossible to ignore.

Killing low-level drug peddlers was like shooting fish in a barrel. She'd killed more losers in the last two weeks than she had the whole year previous. That would be the *opposite* of progress.

But was it all bad?

She smiled to herself, remembering the wreath of fingers she'd hung on the door of the last surviving rival kingpin's captains. It was a small wreath. Sixteen digits, generously spaced. The urban legends she heard about herself had it described as a full-sized wreath, but that would take a *lot* of fingers.

Still, the wreath was a stroke of genius. 'Tis the season...

Hilarious.

She snorted a laugh.

"What are you laughing at?" asked Louis.

She cleared her throat. "Hm? Nothing."

He shook his head and continued playing a video game on his computer.

Stephanie frowned.

Then there's Louis. Handsome and virile at first glance— like so many powerful men's coddled progeny—he'd turned out to be a weak-minded man-child playing Scarface. Worse, he felt invincible now, thanks to her talents. Sure, he paid well, but she didn't enjoy feeling like the spineless king's pet dragon.

In addition, she'd realized too late that working for Louis meant revealing herself to him. He knew what she was.

She didn't like that *at all.*

One of the men Louis kept around to flatter him popped

his head into the office. Most of the guys working for the organization answered directly to Pirro. They were the ones with the dead eyes and questionable tattoos. Then there were one or two who looked like summer interns; they'd followed Louis from the distribution center to his dry cleaning headquarters, all the while catering to his every whim. *Irony Dry Cleaning* was Louis' legitimate front business, and as many of the transactions were cash, served useful for laundering money as well.

"Pirro's going to take care of the old person disco," said the kid at the door.

Louis shrugged. "Okay."

For an answer, the man tapped the door frame twice with his palm and left.

Stephanie scowled. She'd tailed Seamus once to what turned out to be an underground club for old people. She thought it was some sort of money-making scheme, but it belonged to his girlfriend. What was her name...?

Jackie.

"What's this about an old person disco?" she asked.

Louis shrugged without taking his eyes from his computer screen. "Pirro's handling it."

"But why?"

"He says we need the building back. It used to be my father's. I had a club there for a while. We had ice luges for doing shots and—"

"Why do you need it back?"

The growing excitement in Louis expression snuffed out like a light. He'd probably wanted to talk more about ice luges. "I don't know, Pirro said so."

"He's going to kill her? The lady who owns the club?"

"I dunno."

"Why didn't you ask me to do it?"

Louis's tongue hung from his mouth as he pounded on

the keyboard. His character shot some sort of zombie creature into hamburger. "I don't think I need you to kill an old lady."

Stephanie grimaced.

This is getting worse.

If something happened to Seamus's girlfriend and Declan discovered *she* worked for the group responsible, he'd never forgive her.

She took a deep breath. "I need you to not kill the disco lady."

"What?"

"Don't kill the disco lady. I need you to leave her alone."

Louis's video game character took a battle axe to the head and collapsed. Louis turned, eyes blazing. "You made me die."

"Sorry. I need you not to kill the disco lady."

"Why?"

"She's a friend of a friend."

Louis squinted one eye, looking at her as if she had lost her mind.

Frustration growing, Stephanie crossed her legs and folded her hands neatly on her thigh. "Look. I'm asking you, *nicely*, as a favor to me—the woman who single-handedly wiped out your enemy—not to kill this woman."

"You haven't got to the main guy. You've killed two—"

"Three."

Louis's brow crinkled into a knot. "There were only sixteen fingers."

"Yeah, I didn't get the wreath idea until after the first one."

His eyes softened and his mouth opened, breath escaping like he'd just been told her friend's daughter didn't make the cheerleading squad. "Awww. Too bad. It could have been a little bigger."

She shrugged. "Live and learn. Actually, that reminds me—have you looked into the mole?"

"The what?"

Stephanie closed her eyes so Louis wouldn't see them roll. The first man she'd dispatched under his employ had surprised her two days after she met Louis. No one should have known who she was or that she'd been hired to kill the rival boss. Yet forty-eight hours into their partnership, there lurked a clumsy goon in the shadowy corner near her office. Unfortunately for him, he prowled in darkness *provided* by Stephanie for the express purpose of catching potential intruders. She knew her enemies would consider the burnt bulb in that area serendipitous. All she had to do was be prepared whenever she turned that one corner.

She'd been prepared. The goon had been surprised. Disposing of a man in her office parking lot was not ideal, so she'd disposed of the body quickly and without flair. For the next two hits, she'd had the time to harvest a few wreath-making souvenirs.

Now she *owed* this other drug lord a visit. *If only—*

"You haven't told me who the other kingpin is. Did you figure out who he is?" asked Louis.

If only she knew.

Stephanie felt her shoulders slump. She hadn't found him yet. She didn't realize no one knew the identity of the rival bigwig until she'd killed three of his soldiers. Three chances to torture the information out of people, lost forever.

"You didn't tell me he was a mystery man," she grumbled.

"Everyone knows that."

"I'm not a drug dealer, moron, how would I know?"

Louis's expression tightened. She'd forgotten the cardinal rule of Louis: *Never let him know what an idiot he is.*

"Well, too bad. Disco lady has to die," he spat, turning his attention back to his screen.

Stephanie felt rage bubbling inside her. There were no

less than six things on his desk, from his Maserati keys to his stupid pewter University of Florida alligator statue, that she could use to kill him before he had time to shoot another zombie.

Her problem was the men outside his office. Even if she killed every one of them, the gunfire would bring another twenty running. An inbred army of swamp trash worked for Pirro at the compound. Half of them lived here.

That's probably why they want Jackie's club. The compound was getting cramped as Pirro ramped up to take over more corners.

She stood, and the abrupt action made Louis swivel, leaning back in his office chair as if trying to keep his face far from her reach. He looked frightened.

"I'm telling you, *do not kill that woman*," she said through gritted teeth.

Louis's bottom lip thrust out like a scolded child's.

"But I don't really know anything about it. This is Pirro's thing."

"So you're *not* the boss? I'm sorry. I'd been under the impression *you* were the boss. Like your father was."

There. I did it.

She'd pushed the emergency *you're not your father* button.

Louis's cheek twitched. "Pirro!"

No answer came from the other room.

He stood and yelled again. "Pirro!"

The man who had stopped by earlier poked his head in the door once more.

"What's up boss?"

"Where's Pirro?"

"He's off doin' that thing."

"The disco?"

The man nodded.

Louis looked at Stephanie.

"*Call him,*" she growled.

Louis scowled and pointed at the man in the doorway. "Call him!"

The man nodded and pulled his phone from his pocket.

"Went to voicemail."

"Why?"

"No signal out there."

Louis again turned to Stephanie. "No signal."

"I can hear him." She snatched her purse from the chair and headed for the door.

"Where are you going?" asked Louis.

"Home."

She pushed past the man with the phone in his hand and walked through the door. Slipping a hand into her purse as she strode down the hall, she realized her gun was missing.

She'd left it at the office.

Stupid.

She didn't breathe again until she entered her car.

Louis wasn't a problem—she could debone him like a chicken. Pirro, on the other hand, never warmed to her charms. Even her finger wreath didn't make him happy.

He wanted her gone.

She suspected Pirro was responsible for the man hiding in her office's shadows, so he had to be twice as unhappy with her now that his assassin had gone missing. When Pirro finished exploiting Louis's father's name and connections, she suspected someone would be hiding in Louis's shadows as well.

Today, she'd been worried that Pirro's men wouldn't let her leave and now she wasn't prepared for a war. She knew the compound was a danger zone for her, and still she'd forgotten her gun. Hunting untrained thugs, whose deaths wouldn't even be properly investigated by the police, had made her lazy as a zoo-fed lioness.

She scanned the parking lot. Pirro's car was missing.

He's already on his way to Jackie's.

She had to protect Jackie for Declan.

She turned the ignition of her candy apple red Dodge Viper.

This was the problem with relationships. You cared for one person, and next thing you knew, you had to look after the people *they* cared about and *blah, blah, blah.*

Exiting on to the dirt road that led from the compound, Stephanie watched her rearview to be sure no one followed her.

She was clear.

Time to think.

Bobbing her head from side to side she considered a few options for her next move. First, she had to save Jackie. She knew the disco was in the middle of nowhere and relatively indefensible against Pirro's blood-thirsty gang of dirtballs. Without her, Jackie didn't stand a chance. Even Seamus would get himself killed in this situation. The old man was getting older.

If she saved Jackie, Declan would be grateful. Maybe he'd see she was changing for him.

That's all he ever wanted from her.

She was sure.

CHAPTER TWELVE

"Find anything interesting?" asked Declan as he and Charlotte headed into the center of Florida. Already the landscape had gone from suburban sprawl to jungle safari.

Charlotte sat fiddling with Ryan Finnegan's phone.

"The phone isn't quite as old as I thought, but old enough that it isn't locked, so that's a plus."

"And it took a charge?"

"A little so far. I'll plug it in again when we get to Jackie's but right now I have about fifteen percent to try and figure..."

Charlotte's voice trailed off.

"Find something?"

"Pictures. A lot of dark, murky pictures of men standing on corners and cars and license plates... I think Ryan was watching drug dealers."

"Why?"

"I don't know. It sure looks like surveillance, though. Like he was watching the corners and keeping a record of things he thought important."

"Maybe he's a cop? DEA?"

"Maybe."

Charlotte continued flipping and the photos switched

from city corners to the interior of a dimly lit saloon. A woman in slouchy clothes sat at the bar looking out the window. Everything in the image was dark except her shock of blonde hair, peeking from beneath her baseball cap. There was something very familiar about her...

"Stephanie."

"What?"

"There's a picture of Stephanie in here."

Declan huffed. "You're *kidding*."

Charlotte flipped through a few more photos. "No. I'm not. It's definitely her."

She held up the screen and Declan removed his attention from the road long enough to gander. Charlotte thought she saw him pale. She sometimes wondered just how traumatic his former romantic relationship with Stephanie had been. He nearly always had a visceral reaction to her presence. Now, just a photo of her made him wan.

She supposed it made sense. People always made jokes about how terrible their mothers-in-law were, but Stephanie's real mother turned out to be a serial killer. Talk about dodging a bullet.

Literally.

"Eh, *might* be her. You can't tell from that blurry mess," he said, but she could tell he was fooling himself.

Charlotte zoomed in on a picture but found the blonde woman's face didn't grow any clearer in the murky photo. It didn't matter. She could feel it in her bones that the woman in the photo was Stephanie. Declan wasn't the only one who suffered visceral reactions to the image of that flaxen viper.

"It's her. I swear that woman haunts my dreams."

Declan laughed. "*Your* dreams? Imagine how I feel."

Charlotte continued to flip through the phone. There were a few more photos taken from the bar. In one, it appeared to be dusk outside, and she recognized the same drug-riddled street corners she'd seen in the earlier photos.

"Does Stephanie do drugs?"

Declan shook his head. "She likes her whiskey but she's never been into drugs. And she had plenty of opportunities—"

Charlotte looked up as Declan cut short.

"What do you mean?"

"What?"

"You said she had plenty of opportunities and then just stopped mid-sentence."

"Oh, I just mean, you know, she grew up hard. Hung out with the wrong people. The woman her mother dumped her on was a train wreck. If she'd wanted to start taking drugs it wouldn't have been that difficult for her to find them."

"Ah. Gotcha." Charlotte watched Declan a moment longer. She couldn't shake the feeling he wasn't being entirely honest with her.

"Can you think of any reason she'd be hanging out in shady bars located near drug corners?"

He shrugged. "Who knows what she's up to at any given moment? She's a criminal defense attorney. Maybe she was meeting a client there."

Charlotte nodded. That wasn't out of the realm of possibility. *Could Ryan be Stephanie's client?* No. The photos were taken from the opposite side of the establishment. She didn't appear to see him.

But what was Ryan's interest in Stephanie? Most of the other photos were of men—boys really—selling drugs or loitering as if waiting for the chance to sell them. There were more photos of that ilk and then a few more of Stephanie. She wore the same clothes but the gap between the pictures made Charlotte check the date stamps. They weren't all taken on the same day. Stephanie had been at that bar more than once wearing the same drab, shapeless clothing.

She could call Stephanie a lot of things, but lousy dresser

wasn't one of them. The girl always looked like she was on her way to a sexy magazine photo shoot.

It was one of the things Charlotte hated most about her.

That, and what appeared to be a laser focus on destroying Charlotte's relationship with Declan.

Charlotte shook her head to clear it of petty jealousy. It was stupid to waste a single second worrying about Stephanie's motives with Declan.

Okay. Done. Back to business.

Charlotte reasoned if the sloppy clothes didn't fit Stephanie's style, they had to be a costume. She was attempting to go unnoticed in that filthy bar.

Stephanie is doing her own surveillance.

That had to be it. Stephanie appeared to be killing time, and nothing said *surveillance* like killing time somewhere you'd rather not be.

Was she working with Ryan?

Maybe. Or maybe Ryan noticed Stephanie because he'd been watching that corner long enough to know she didn't belong. He took photos of her *because* she didn't belong. He may or may not have known where she fit in his puzzle, but he knew she was an interesting piece.

Charlotte resumed flipping and the photos of Stephanie ended. More drug activity appeared. She saw what appeared to be the third or fourth instance of a black Mercedes parked at the curb. One of the boys from the corner was talking to someone inside.

The man in that car must be the boss. Or at least someone a notch up from the kids on the corner. Ryan's camera didn't take the best pictures so there was no way to identify the people in the car.

A few photos later, Ryan's world seemed much happier. There were a few pictures of the beach taken from a high vantage point. She recognized them as views from Ryan's condo.

A young man's image appeared. It was a photo of another photo; she could make out the edges of the frame. It was the photo of Craig, Ryan's son, she'd seen on the table at his condo. The next photo was a piece of paper. A form. She zoomed in.

"An autopsy report," she said aloud.

"What's that?"

"He took a photo of his son's autopsy report. Craig Finnegan." She squinted, trying to read through the coroner's report using the blurry zoom. "Drug overdose."

"He lost his son?"

Charlotte nodded. "Mariska and Darla remembered Ryan when he lived in Pineapple Port. Apparently, his son died and left him money. After that, he moved to the condo we visited. They didn't know how his son died, but it looks like drug overdose."

"That's a shame."

"Hold on...it looks like he died *here*. I thought Ryan's son died out in Silicon Valley where he made his money, but this report was filled out by a Florida coroner."

"Maybe he was visiting his dad when he died."

"Maybe."

Charlotte sat in silence for a moment before beginning to think out loud.

"That would make you crazy."

"Losing a son?"

"And losing a son on your watch. From all accounts, his son was doing very well in California, then he comes here to visit his dad and dies of a drug overdose."

"You're thinking Ryan was trying to find out who sold his son the drugs."

Charlotte nodded. "He's watching the corners like a cop. He's trying to find who's to blame."

"And maybe bring them down."

"And then he goes missing."

"Doesn't seem like much of a mystery why he went missing when you know what he's been up to."

"No. That's what I'm thinking. I think someone noticed Ryan. But why did they go to his house to grab him? Why didn't they just grab him during one of his visits to their neck of the woods?"

"Maybe they thought he was a cop? That he had a partner watching somewhere near by?"

"Maybe. Heck, for all we know maybe he *is* a cop."

Charlotte ran out of photos and began to search through the phone for anything else that might be useful. She'd just noticed a few voice messages when the phone went black.

"Shoot. I ran out of juice."

"Well, you made some good progress. Now you know Ryan is probably the victim of his own attempt at vigilante justice. Or a cop."

Charlotte   sighed.   "And   probably   dead."

CHAPTER THIRTEEN

Charlotte and Declan cruised the dirt road that led to Jackie's club. Seamus had told them to watch for a bullet-riddled alligator crossing sign standing on the side of the road, twenty feet from the entrance.

Handy *and* disturbing.

The club came into view, a large square building with a covered parking area attached to one side. A darkened neon sign hung over the only visible entrance. Charlotte could make out the outline of what looked like a disco dancer with his finger pointing to the sky. His opposite hand rested on the small of his arched back, as if he'd just pulled something and had reached for the pain. Beside him, it read, *Slipped Disc'o.*

"I don't see Seamus's car," said Declan. They circled the club and parked on the opposite side. "That figures."

Charlotte gathered Mariska's charge cord and Ryan's phone, figuring she could glean a few more insights from the phone on the way back home.

They headed inside to find Jackie cleaning a whiskey glass, standing behind an ornate, dark-wood bar. Her head snapped up and she put a hand on her chest.

"Oh jeeze, I didn't hear you drive up. You scared me."

Jackie tucked away the glass and walked to the opposite side of the bar. "Where's Seamus? He said he might bring you along."

"Your guess is as good as ours," said Charlotte.

Jackie shook her head, smiling. "That man would be late to his own funeral."

Declan's mouth hooked to the right. "I think he was once. Have him tell you that story."

"Do you mind if I plug in this phone? It's dead and I need to juice it."

"Oh sure, give it to me. There's a plug right behind the bar here."

Jackie plugged in Ryan's phone while Charlotte's and Declan's gazes swept the disco. A large dancefloor complete with a DJ stage occupied most of the center of the enormous building. Wooden benches and booths flanked the center. Her impressive bar occupied most of the right wall. A disco ball the size of a small planet hung from the ceiling, and in the shadowy recesses of the room, Charlotte spotted gun-shaped equipment awaiting the chance to fill the room with laser beams and disco-ball-refracted sparkles.

She whistled. "This place is pretty impressive."

Declan nodded. "It's bigger than I imagined."

"It used to be a shipping depot of some sort," said Jackie, overhearing Declan's comment as she returned to them. "The company went out of business, someone tried to turn the building into a dance club and failed, and then I bought it for a song."

Charlotte grunted. "Not a big surprise it went out of business. This isn't the most accessible location for a trucking company or a bar."

Jackie grinned. "But it's a great location for an underground club."

Declan clapped his hands together. "So what's up? Seamus asked me to swing by and help him with some trouble."

Jackie lifted a hand to her cheek, head shaking. "I don't know. Maybe I'm overreacting. But too many things are happening all at once."

"Like what?" asked Charlotte.

"For one, I keep finding dead animals on the property. A skunk, an armadillo...they look like they were hit by cars, but they're not being hit in the parking lot. It's like someone is finding them on the road and bringing them here."

"Maybe an animal is dragging them here?" suggested Charlotte.

Declan nodded. "Or kids. It sounds like a kid's prank."

Jackie swept a hand through the air. "There aren't any kids around here for miles. The ones old enough to drive out here have other things on their minds than leaving dead skunks on my doorstep."

Charlotte clucked her tongue. "I'd find it odd if a kid nowadays looked up from his phone long enough to pull a prank."

"Exactly," agreed Jackie, chuckling.

Charlotte found Declan staring at her.

"What?"

"You know you've been living in Pineapple Port so long, you *sound* like a retiree, right?"

Laughing, Charlotte felt an embarrassed flush spread across her cheeks. She knew it was true. "Anything else?"

"A lot. Twice, men have come asking to buy the place. The first were real slick-looking, lawyerly—all fancy suits and smiling faces. When I turned them down they were nice about it. The second two..." Jackie grimaced.

"Scary?"

"Very scary. Like something out of a crime movie. One man looked Hispanic, but he had strawberry-blond hair that didn't seem to go with the rest of him. His friend was muscly and didn't do anything but stare. When I turned them down, they told me their boss *wouldn't be pleased*."

"Did they say who their boss was?"

Jackie shook her head. "That's what I'm afraid of... that phase three is meeting the boss."

"Do you know why they want the place?" asked Declan.

"No. They never say. I asked them, but they ignored me."

A phone rang and Jackie glanced behind her.

"That's the office phone. It's probably Seamus letting me know he'll be late. Come back with me. I have some papers I found in the parking lot that I think the second lot of visitors dropped. There might be some information you can use to figure out who they are."

Declan and Charlotte followed Jackie to the office. By the time they arrived, the phone had stopped ringing. Jackie shrugged.

"He'll try my cell if it was him."

She rustled through some papers and retrieved a yellowing, folded sheet of thick paper. Unfolding it, she laid it out flat and tried to smooth it with her palm.

"It looks like a map," said Declan.

Charlotte nodded. "But it's so scribbly. All these connected boxes on this side...and look at this long stripe that goes to—what does that say?"

Declan squinted. "Does it say something? I'm not sure that's even writing."

Charlotte looked up at Jackie. "Are you sure the men dropped this?"

"No. Could have been anyone. It just happened to show up on the same day, so I kept it. Do you want to see the skunk?"

Charlotte laughed. "No, I think we're good. I don't think fingerprints stick to skunks."

Declan straightened. "Did you hear that? Sounded like a car door."

"Seamus," said Jackie.

She sounded relieved.

CHAPTER FOURTEEN

Stephanie stomped her brakes and the Viper skidded three feet down the dirt road.

She'd seen a flash of metal through the trees.

Another car appeared ahead of her, pulling into the parking lot of Jackie's bar.

She'd caught up to Pirro and his thugs before they had time to hurt Jackie.

Stephanie pulled a pair of binoculars from her glove compartment and stepped from her car to gain a better view.

She needed to make sure it was them. If the car ahead of her belonged to Jackie, she wasn't sure how to explain her presence.

Hi Jackie, I'm an old friend of Declan and Seamus. Remember me? I thought I'd swing by and find out how easy it would be for a red-headed drug prince to kill you...

The binoculars came into focus. The car didn't belong to Jackie. She didn't know what Jackie drove, but she knew it wasn't a silver Impala with stylized flames across the hood. Only one cretin drove *that* car.

Pirro.

With dark skin, pale red hair and a face like a chewed

piece of gum, the last thing that man needed was a flashy car to draw attention.

Yet there it was.

She watched as two other men hopped from the Impala. One lit a cigarette. The other drew a gun and headed toward the club.

Here we go.

She hadn't planned on everything happening so fast.

Stephanie looked back at her car and remembered with renewed dismay that she'd forgotten her gun. Usually, she kept a spare in the trunk, but she'd taken the Glock inside her office to clean the day before.

Stupid, stupid.

It wasn't like her to make such a moronic mistake. Maybe it was her subconscious trying to tell her something.

Maybe I should get a shrink. Get a little therapy, get in touch with my feelings, and then kill the doctor so he or she doesn't rat on me...

Maybe she was sick of killing Louis's enemies, but right now she *longed* to kill Pirro.

Kicking off her Louboutins, she winced as one skidded along the dirt road and slipped into a muddy little moat.

Seven hundred dollar shoes. I could have been a little less dramatic.

Breaking into a sprint, she removed the jacket of her skirt-suit and hung it on a broken branch as she passed. She jerked up her skirt to keep it from restricting her stride. The gravel road bit into the bottoms of her feet, but she pressed on.

This was her chance to do something good. Something Declan could appreciate.

Plus she *really* wanted to kill Pirro. She felt very in touch with her feelings on that one.

The man with the gun was nearing Jackie's door. There was no way to get by Pirro and his smoking partner *and* get to the door without being spotted. Several feet short from the parking lot, Stephanie stopped and leaned over, slipping her fingers into the swamp mud.

Does Declan have any idea the things I do for him?

She smeared the mud on her face and arms. She couldn't bear to slap mud on her Burberry blouse. Unbuttoning it, she limped onto the asphalt, her lacy bra exposed, her hair rumpled to cascade across her face.

"Help," she said, walking toward the smoking man. She tried to call loud enough to catch the attention of the man about to enter the building, but he opened the door and disappeared inside without turning.

Shoot. Have to make this quick.

"Hey." The smoking man spotted her. He knocked the side of his fist against the car door to catch the driver's attention before walking towards her.

"Eh, Chica, you look like you could use some help."

Stephanie peered through her hair at the leering smile on the man's face. He was as likely to help her as she was likely to let him live another ten minutes.

Pirro popped his head through the passenger window.

"Hey baby, what—"

Stephanie watched the leer drop from Pirro's face. His eyes grew wide.

"Chewie, don't! That's that crazy—"

Still grinning, Chewie turned to better hear Pirro. "What?"

Bad move, Chewie.

The moment his attention diverted, Stephanie lunged forward like a cobra. She snatched Chewie's gun from his waist band, firing it into his gut as she pulled it from his belt.

He'd felt her arrive a second too late. His head turned, his mouth forming a large O as he doubled over and fell to the ground, clutching his stomach.

Stephanie stepped aside to let him fall and strode toward Pirro, gun raised and pointed at his gaping mouth. He whipped back into his car.

It pained her, but she made a judgment call.

"You better run, Pirro. You touch your gun and I will make sure you die last and *slow*."

Pirro knew her reputation well enough not to doubt her. He hit the gas and rolled into the adjoining field, making a wide U-turn back toward the road.

Tracing his progress with her gun, Stephanie gritted her teeth. She'd wanted to kill Pirro, but the gun she'd pulled from Chewie only had five bullets left, tops. He carried an archaic six-shooter. Obviously liked to pretend he was an old-time gunslinger. A purist.

She could have easily sunk the remaining five bullets into the Impala without touching Pirro, who had a gun, or guns, of his own... and knowledge of Chewie's weapon of choice. As afraid of her as he was, he knew she wasn't bulletproof.

A shot and a scream rang out and Stephanie swiveled her attention to the dance club. For the first time she noticed a car parked on the opposite side of the building.

She recognized it.

It was Declan's.

Stephanie bolted for the club. Behind her, another gunshot rang and she heard something wiz by her head. Pirro had taken a potshot at her on her way down the road

Such   a   jackass.

CHAPTER FIFTEEN

Charlotte cocked her head and heard what sounded like a chair sliding across the club's wooden floor.

"Here he comes. Sounds like he already took a seat at the bar."

Jackie laughed. "I wouldn't be surprised."

Declan took a step toward the partially closed door of the office.

Suddenly, the world around Charlotte burst into a tornado of motion.

The door flung inward. Declan dodged to avoid being struck by it. As he twisted, a man appeared in the doorway and raised his arm, leveling a gun at Jackie's face.

Charlotte fought to free her body from the shock of the commotion, diving toward Jackie as the crack of the weapon echoed through the small room. Jackie screamed and collapsed beneath Charlotte's tackle. Her left foot shot forward, punching the back of Declan's knee, causing him to buckle backwards. Something hot bit Charlotte's shoulder. It felt as though she'd been stung by a wasp.

A wasp made of lava.

An odd thought crossed her mind.

Television *lies.*

On TV, gun-shot people claimed the wound didn't even hurt, thanks to the shock of the event.

That was a lie.

Her shoulder sang with pain.

Landing on Jackie, Charlotte looked up in time to see Declan's legs collapsing. He'd been clipped hard by Jackie's fall.

She thrust her arm upward and shoved his butt skyward. It was all he needed. He regained his balance.

What next?

Charlotte realized she didn't know what to do. Her instinct had been to push Jackie from the path of the bullet, but what did she do once she was *on her friend* and *on the floor?* Television never showed that part. Now they were both on the ground, sitting ducks for the next bullet. Assuming the intruder's gun had any power at all, he could shoot through them both with one bullet.

While she appreciated economy of effort, she wasn't rooting for the man to save ammunition today.

She saw Jackie's mouth move but heard nothing. Her ears were ringing. Jackie looked terrified.

Charlotte turned toward the intruder and watched Declan crack the man across the wrist with what looked like a *real* karate chop. The gun fell to the ground, blasting a second time as it tumbled. Even Charlotte's ringing ears heard the bullet strike the wall above her head. She ducked, cringing and pushing Jackie's head lower.

Though in mortal danger, on the upside, she wasn't totally deaf—or at least she wasn't *before* the second shot. Now she wasn't so sure. Though she thought she detected the muffled sounds of Jackie growing increasingly hysterical.

Let's try this again.

The man snarled and struck at Declan, who swept his arm to the right, deflecting the blow. He tagged the assailant with his left fist, but as the man's head snapped back, he kicked out with his leg, catching the side of Declan's shin. The two of them exchanged a flurry of blows, each blocking the other's punch or kick with one of his own.

Short of an action movie, Charlotte had never seen two people fight so furiously before. It was almost as if a director had choreographed the battle. Stunned by the violent dance, it took her a second to realize Declan might appreciate some help.

"Stay down," she said to Jackie, knowing that between the gun shots and the screaming, there wasn't much chance she'd been heard. Considering the panic on Jackie's expression, she wasn't too worried her friend would try to rise any time soon.

Charlotte scrambled to her feet.

"Get the gun," roared Declan.

Charlotte perked. *I heard that!*

How Declan was able to see what she was doing while playing some sort of savage patty-cake game, she didn't know.

Good idea, though.

She searched for the gun, unsure where it had skittered after the second shot. Spotting the weapon near the file cabinet, she reached for it, only to have her hand stomped on by the intruder.

Seems their foe could also multitask.

She howled in pain.

Declan rushed the man, sending him slamming back into the door jamb. The force shifted the man's foot from Charlotte's fingers to the gun, kicking the weapon across the room. Charlotte scrambled after it. She'd nearly reached it when the two fighting men stumbled back in the opposite direction, grappling and twirling as they struggled for power. Jackie squealed and scrambled behind the desk. Declan's heel hit the gun and it spun into the desk leg before ricocheting back toward the file cabinet.

Charlotte rolled out of the way to avoid being trampled.

Spotting the gun on the opposite side of the room, she again crawled toward it, only to have the battle switch directions, blocking her progress.

On her hands and knees she peered up at the wrestling men. "Oh come *on*."

Pleased to find she could hear her own complaining, she dove for the gun and grabbed it, hastily pointing it back at its owner.

She never had a chance to scream *Freeze!* or *Stop or I'll shoot!* or any of the other cool things she'd remember shouting when she collected her dramatic private-eye exploits into a best-selling memoir.

Declan robbed her of the chance.

No sooner had she raised the gun, than Declan slammed the other man's head to his knee. As the man bounced back to an upright position, stunned and wobbling, Declan side-kicked him through the door. Splinters of wood exploded as the man plummeted to the dance floor outside, landing spread-eagled and unconscious.

Possibly dead.

Charlotte wasn't sure how anyone survived having their head plowed into a kneecap before being face-kicked through what appeared to have once been a pretty solid door.

Charlotte watched as Declan rushed to the man, checking to be sure he'd neutralized his enemy.

Since when could Declan fight like that?

Declan turned to her, his eyes still wild with intensity, chest rising and falling with the exertion of his battle. She spotted the moment he truly focused on her. The fury in his eyes calmed. His expression relaxed. He appeared almost embarrassed.

"We need to find some rope to tie him up," he said.

Charlotte nodded. "We also need to *talk*."

The sound of a car door slamming echoed from the other room.

Jackie yelped as if she'd snapped from a quick nap. Charlotte jumped. She'd almost forgotten Jackie was there.

Declan grabbed the gun from Charlotte's hand and ran from the room.

CHAPTER SIXTEEN

Declan cracked open the front door and peered outside. A barefooted woman running toward the building stopped and held up a gun.

Stephanie.

He opened the door and pointed his own gun at her. They stood, locked in their stalemate.

"Stephanie," he said.

"Declan."

"Are you responsible for this?"

She smiled. "The guy who went in there? Uh, *no*. That one—" She motioned over her shoulder with her gun. Declan leaned to the left and spotted a man on the ground fifty yards behind her, one hand waving in the air, the other gripping his bleeding gut. "That one was me," she added.

He lowered his weapon. "Is he armed?"

She scoffed. "What am I, stupid?"

"He's not going anywhere?"

"He'll be lucky if he doesn't bleed out in another five minutes."

Declan sighed. "Who are they? The one in here was trained."

"Drug thugs. They work for Louis Beaumont. Sort of. I suspect he works for *them*, but he doesn't know that. He's playing drug lord dress-up."

"Any relation to Victor Beaumont?"

"His son. Not exactly a chip off the old block."

"And you? Do you work for them?"

Stephanie hooked her mouth to the side. "Would you believe I'm recently retired?"

He shook his head and glanced at the dying man in the parking lot. His hand still hovered in the air, dropping lower by the second.

"I'll call an ambulance. I suppose you'd better come in. I have to check on the other guy."

Declan felt someone approaching and turned with his gun raised. Charlotte stopped and held up her hands.

"Whoa."

He lowered the gun. "Sorry."

Charlotte peered out the door and scowled. "What is *she* doing here?"

Stephanie waved, gun still in her hand. "Hi, girlfriend."

Declan frowned. "I don't exactly know yet. I need to get this guy tied up."

"Already done," said Charlotte, as Stephanie and Declan entered. Charlotte scowled and craned her neck to peer around them. "Is that a guy in the parking lot?"

Stephanie nodded as she walked past Charlotte. "My bad."

Declan glanced at the man Charlotte had tied up. She'd tied him to the bar foot rail. It didn't look like he'd be going anywhere, even if he happened to wake up.

Declan turned his attention to Stephanie, who'd perched herself at the bar. "What is all this? Why does Louis Beaumont want this place bad enough to kill for it?"

"Your guess is as good as mine. Something to do with drugs, I imagine. They're sort of one-minded that way."

"Who's Louis Beaumont?" asked Charlotte.

"A drug dealer," said Declan.

Stephanie held up a finger. "He prefers to be called a *businessman*, thank you very much."

Charlotte scowled. "You're working for him?"

"Not after I shot his guy, I think." Stephanie blew her hair out of her face. "I was over it anyway."

Declan glanced toward the front door. "We need to call an ambulance."

"Oh let me," said Stephanie grabbing the phone on the bar. She stopped and stared at the screen.

"Is that *me*?" she asked, turning the screen away from her to face Declan.

Declan looked at the screen and recognized the photo Charlotte had shown him earlier of Stephanie sitting at a bar.

Stephanie didn't wait for an answer and turned the screen back to herself.

"This angle. I know who took this shot. He's at Louis's dry cleaning right now."

"What?" Charlotte took a step forward. "Ryan Finnegan is mixed up in this?"

"Not on purpose. Last I saw him he was tied to a chair. Unless he's into that sort of thing and then maybe it is on purpose."

Charlotte looked at Declan, who turned, scowling at Stephanie.

"You didn't think to free him?"

Stephanie's eyes grew wide. "Little ole me? How could I free a kidnapped man from a drug dealer?"

Declan's jaw tightened. "Stephanie, I swear to—"

She held up her hands. "It was none of my business. I've got my own issues. If you wouldn't mind, I'd like you to take a second to realize that if it hadn't been for me you'd all be dead by now." She glanced at the unconscious man tied to the foot rail of the bar. "You might have handled one but you wouldn't have handled three."

Declan did the math. "Three? I count two. Him and gut wound out there."

"You forgot Pirro."

"Where's he?"

Stephanie shrugged. "On his way for reinforcements, I imagine."

The door swung open and Declan and Stephanie both drew their weapons.

"Charlotte, there's some drunk out in the parking lot—" Mariska covered her head with her hands. "Don't shoot!"

Stephanie's eyes rolled in Charlotte's direction as she lowered her weapon. "I assume she's one of yours."

"I think that man might be hurt," said Darla entering a moment later. She stopped and stared at Mariska, who remained balled up like an armadillo standing on one foot. She looked at Charlotte. "What's that all about?"

Charlotte sighed. "A misunderstanding. What are you two doing here?"

"We followed you—" Darla pointed. "Is that a man tied to the bar?"

Charlotte nodded.

Scowling, Darla continued. "We wanted to see the club and ask Jackie why she never invited us here. Where is she?"

Charlotte thrust a thumb in the direction of the office. "Hiding behind the desk in there."

Darla strode past the others, pausing a moment to ogle at the destroyed office door before stepping inside.

"We have to get out of here," said Declan.

Charlotte walked over to Mariska, encouraging her to uncurl. Mariska peeked from under her hands to find the weapons gone. Her shoulders unbunched.

Darla and a pale, shaky Jackie walked from the office,

Darla's arm wrapped around Jackie's shoulder.

"What did you do to her?" asked Darla.

Mariska scowled at Charlotte. "Young lady, you tell me what's going on here right now."

Charlotte put her hand on her chest. "You think *I'm* responsible for all this?"

Stephanie wiped the prints from the gun in her hand with her shirt and motioned towards the parking lot. "This is his gun. I'm going to put it back in his hand. He won't tell the cops anything. Just say you found him out there."

"How do you know he won't say anything?" asked Charlotte.

"Two reasons. First, men like him don't talk to cops. There are things in his world a lot scarier than jail." Stephanie fell silent.

"And the second reason?" prompted Charlotte.

"Oh. Right. He'll be dead."

Jackie leaned on the bar, panting, as Darla stroked her hair. "Your dance club is lovely."

Jackie swallowed. "Thank you."

"You're not hurt, are you?" asked Mariska. As she took a step toward Darla and Jackie, she noticed the man tied to the bottom of the bar for the first time.

She yipped, hand on her heart as she gave him wide berth.

"They're *everywhere.*"

The front door slammed as Seamus burst in, calling Jackie's name.

Again, Declan and Stephanie raised and lowered their guns. Jackie dislodged herself from Darla's embrace and scrambled into Seamus's waiting arms.

"I just cleaned this thing," said Stephanie, again wiping her prints from the gun.

"What in the name of St. Patrick is goin' on in here?"

asked Seamus attempting to soothe his frantic girlfriend.

The roar of a muscle car growled outside.

"That would be Pirro," said Stephanie, picking up the newly cleaned gun once more. "I give up."

"Everyone behind the bar, now!" roared Declan.

CHAPTER SEVENTEEN

Mariska and Darla scurried behind the bar. Jackie scrambled to the office. Seamus bolted to the front door, locked it, and dropped a large metal bar across it.

"That's handy," said Declan, admiring the thickness of the door's draw bar. "Is the extra security thanks to these goons?"

Seamus shook his head. "Nah. Jackie worried about kids breaking into the place and cleaning out her booze. They could drink the place dry by the time the cops ever got here. I made sure the place seals up like a castle."

Declan dialed 9-1-1 and then looked at his phone.

"I've got no signal."

"There's no tower out here. There's a landline in the—"

"The phone line's dead," wailed Jackie as she stumbled over the splintered office door on her way to join Darla and Mariska behind the bar.

Declan scowled at his uncle. "They thought to cut the line that fast?"

Seamus's expression belied his concern. "I guess they're familiar with the place?"

"Did I mention one of them is the nephew of Diego

Rodríguez?" asked Stephanie from her seat at the bar.

Declan felt the blood drain from his cheeks. He turned to Seamus.

"Point me to other possible weak spots."

"There's a back door. Stays locked as a rule but check it. I'll take care of the window in the bathroom."

Jackie's head popped up from behind the bar like a wild-eyed gopher's. "Shouldn't she be back here with us instead of sitting there drinking my bourbon?" she asked, pointing at Stephanie.

Declan glanced at his ex, who'd grabbed a giant bottle of Bulleit and poured herself a shot. He motioned to the bar.

"You have a weapon. Can I trust you to watch over them?"

Stephanie glanced down where the three ladies huddled and shrugged. "Within reason."

Declan beckoned to Charlotte and the two of them jogged to the small, makeshift kitchen.

"How can I help?" asked Charlotte.

Declan eyed the industrial-sized refrigerator. "Help me push this in front of the door."

He gave one side a yank to pull it out from the wall. Charlotte took a position beside him and on the count of three, they shoved in unison. The giant metal box moved a few inches.

Charlotte moaned and reached for her shoulder.

Declan instinctively touched her and she jerked away as if in pain. His fingers glistened with blood.

"You're bleeding. Hold still."

She snorted. "Easy for you to say."

He inspected her shoulder.

"It looks like you were shot. Grazed. Why didn't you tell me?"

"I'll be honest, with all the commotion I forgot. It only

hurt right after it happened. Will I live?"

He smiled. "Just a flesh wound."

"Oh good. I hear that in the movies all the time. That means I'm fine."

Declan held his smile a moment longer, though inside he didn't feel very cheery. They were trapped in a box in the middle of nowhere and his girlfriend had already been shot.

"You look ill," said Charlotte.

"I'm worried." He didn't know why he thought he could hide his concern from her. She was the most intuitive person he'd ever met.

Charlotte put her good shoulder against the refrigerator. "I'm *fine*. On three. One-two-*three!*" On *three* they pushed and the refrigerator moved another few inches.

"I do have a question or two for you, though," added Charlotte.

Declan grimaced. "I was afraid you'd say that. One-two-*three*—"

Shove.

The unit slid half-way in front of the locked and barricaded back door.

Charlotte braced herself for the next big push. "How did you fight that guy like you've been spending weekends training with the UFC? One-two-*three*—"

Shove.

Declan swallowed. "There are a couple things I need to tell you. One-two-*three*—"

Shove.

They gave the unit a last mighty push and it moved into place, blocking entry through the back door as best it could.

Charlotte brushed her hands together, staring holes through him. "You were saying?"

Declan inhaled and released a deep breath. "When I was eighteen, I was sort of a mess. Angry at the world about my mom's disappearance and my father leaving. Seamus hooked me up with a job in Miami for a while. Sort of an underground drug task force called The Honey Badgers."

Charlotte laughed. "The Honey Badgers? Seriously? I thought Stephanie was kidding."

"It was around the time that *honey badger don't care* meme came out. It was silly. Anyway, Seamus figured their training regimen would be good for me. Knock the angry out of me, so to speak."

"They taught you how to fight?"

He nodded and tried to hold her gaze. He knew if he looked away she'd dig even deeper.

"Why didn't you ever tell me about this?"

Declan stared at the floor and sighed. "I don't know. To be honest I've pushed that part of my life out of my head. It isn't something I'm proud of and I don't like to think about it."

"How long did you do it?" she asked.

"Not long."

"Something went wrong?"

Declan nodded. "That's a nice way to put it. The man who ran the program, Mateo, was supposed to combat drugs on our shores, but decided to take things up a few notches and fly us to South America. The Honey Badgers was a civilian shadow organization, so there wasn't any real oversight. I didn't like the way he handled things."

"They sound like mercenaries. Why would Seamus get you involved?"

"He didn't know how bad it would get."

"So you refused to go to South America?"

"No. I went. But soon after we scattered and it was over."

He could tell Charlotte knew a larger South America story had been tossed aside by his one-sentence summary.

"So...Stephanie said the man training Louis's men is an ex-Honey Badger. You told her about your time there?"

And there it is. The bit he hadn't wanted to share right now.

Declan's voice caught in his throat as he croaked his painfully honest answer. "She was there."

"*Stephanie* was a Honey Badger?"

He nodded.

Charlotte took a moment to absorb this new information.

"Why can't I get the picture out of my head of you two running sweaty and half-dressed through the jungles of South America with AK-47s in your hands?."

"You really have to watch less television."

She smiled and patted him on the shoulder. "You know, that makes sense. It explains her obsession with you. You've been through a lot more than just growing up together and dating for a while."

"I suppose." His eye drifted to a first aid kit mounted to the wall. "We need to patch that wound of yours."

"Is it bleeding?"

"Not bad. It's just a graze but you don't want it getting infected."

Careful to avoid her shoulder, Declan wrapped his arms around Charlotte and held her to him, talking low in her ear.

"You stay near me until we're out of this, okay?"

She pushed back far enough to plant her lips on his.

"I'd be crazy not to, now that I know you're a trained assassin."

He chuckled and pushed away his fear that she'd realize her   guess   had   been   close   to   the   mark.

CHAPTER EIGHTEEN

Charlotte and Declan explored the few offshoot rooms of the disco, searching for weaknesses. Because the building had once served as a shipping warehouse, there were blessedly few points of entry to secure. The structure was built like a giant shoebox.

"We're getting lucky with the windows and doors here, Rambo," said Charlotte as she peered into a closet.

"Don't start that," said Declan.

"You prefer Mr. Bond?"

Declan tried to flash her a disapproving stare but a smile split his stony expression. "I should know better than to tell you anything."

Charlotte giggled and glanced into Jackie's tiny office. It wasn't difficult, with the door exploded on the ground at her feet. Nerves danced in her stomach. Not only were they under attack, but now she dreaded discovering more about Declan's past with The Honey Badgers. She knew her teasing and nervous laughter would only distract her from the gravity of the situation for so long.

Office clear, she returned to the main room. As she passed the desk, the strange piece of paper Jackie had found in her parking lot caught her eye. A menagerie of meaningless squares scribbled on it, but...now something about the shapes' configuration felt more familiar than it had upon first inspection.

Charlotte stared at the drawing. *What is it?* Something about this grid—

She sucked in a breath.

It isn't a grid. It's rooms.

No wonder the shapes felt more familiar. The boxes represented the rooms she'd been searching for the last ten minutes. Having explored the club, it became obvious the paper was a rough map of the disco. She recognized the smaller boxes representing the bathrooms, the large one for the dance floor...

The remaining confusing bit was a skinny strip that led away from the building constructed by two dashed lines. *A road?* Maybe they were planning to build a road to the disco. Maybe to use it as a drug warehouse.

That would make sense. The property *was* in the middle of nowhere, where the occupants wouldn't have to worry about too many prying eyes.

The road led to another box. *Maybe their current warehouse?*

That second box had another offshoot that led nowhere.

Maybe the lines didn't mean anything.

There wasn't time to speculate on the mapping skills of drug dealers. Charlotte folded the paper into a tight square and stuffed it in her pocket. She wasn't sure why, but it seemed important. Maybe tomorrow—if she lived until tomorrow—she could give it additional thought.

Maybe the men outside wanted the map? She could toss it out the door and they would go away. That would be good. Though the drawing seemed too crude and easy to reproduce for that to be true.

Turning to leave, she ran directly into Declan's broad chest and bounced back. He caught her before she could fall.

"Watch it there, Bumble," he said, using a nickname he'd once labeled her after watching her trip no less than five times in one day.

She blushed, embarrassed. "Hey—I was on my way. I realized—"

Seamus appeared behind Declan and moved to a bank of three small televisions. He pressed a button and the screens flickered to life, presenting the front and back of the club from different angles. Outside, a dark-skinned man with impossibly orange-red hair stepped out of a car with flames on the hood and a backend wrapped in a red tartan plaid. He drew a gun and walked across the parking lot toward the man writhing on the ground.

"He's busy saving his friend. We should go for it now," suggested Seamus.

"He's got a gun," said Declan.

"We have two."

Declan frowned. "You think we should run out there, start a gun battle with him, and then ask everyone to step over his dead body and get in our cars?"

Seamus sniffed. "It's not a terrible idea. He's planning on gunning us down. Shouldn't we get him first?"

Declan shook his head. "There are too many unknowns. For now, we're safer in here. He might grab his friend and leave—"

There was a *pop!* outside and all gazes shot to the flickering screens. The redheaded man had his gun pointed at the man on the ground. The man no longer moved.

Charlotte gasped. "Did he just kill his friend?"

"With friends like that..." mumbled Seamus, glancing at Declan. "Still think we don't know his intentions? The longer we wait the better chance his reinforcements will arrive—"

As if on cue, another car rolled into the parking lot.

Charlotte's shoulders slumped. "Well, that window closed quickly."

Declan turned and strode toward the disco area. "They're going to try and shoot their way in. We need to get everyone safe."

Charlotte and Seamus jogged after him.

"Everyone stay behind the bar. That means you too," Declan said, nudging Charlotte toward the others as she exited the office. He glanced at Seamus and then Stephanie. "And you and you."

"Building secure?" asked Stephanie.

Declan nodded. "But another car just arrived."

Stephanie rolled her eyes. "Give me a second to think."

"You can think behind the—"

Gunfire erupted outside. Charlotte had stopped to listen to Declan and Stephanie's conversation and now dropped to a squat, her hands covering her head. Declan pounced on her, covering her like a muscular blanket. She heard a bullet ricochet off something metal and the sound of Mariska screaming.

"Yo! Yo!" screamed a voice outside, followed by a string of profanities. The gunfire ceased. "—the building!" was the last line Charlotte heard.

She dropped her hands from her face as Declan released her.

"Not many got through," said Declan, already standing and surveying the damage. "How is that possible? Isn't this building metal?"

"I had the building reinforced for storms, noise and to keep the air conditioning bills lower," said Jackie from behind the bar. "It's cement block all around, encased by the aluminum sheeting."

"Someone has to tell me what is going on!" roared Darla,

thrusting a finger at Stephanie from her position on the floor. "That one wouldn't tell us anything while you were running around. Just some nonsense about drug dealers."

Charlotte stood. "Stay where you are."

"Who are these people?" asked Mariska, looking terrified. Charlotte wanted to do something to soothe her fears, but all she could think to do was share the truth.

"We think they want Jackie's disco to use for drug distribution."

Darla's eyes bulged. "Are you kidding me? The drug dealers are real?" She looked at Jackie. "Did you know about this?"

Jackie shook her head. "I knew someone wanted to buy the place and that they were being really pushy and a little scary but I never *dreamed* this would happen."

Darla fumbled in her purse and pulled out her phone. "I have to call Frank."

"There's no signal," reminded Jackie.

Darla scowled. "So we're trapped in here with drug dealers shooting at the building?"

"Better than being out there," said Stephanie.

Mariska squinted at Stephanie. "This is your fault somehow. I *know* it."

Stephanie shook her head. "Believe it or not, if I hadn't come you'd all be dead already."

"Okay, okay, bickering isn't going to get us anywhere," said Charlotte, giving Mariska a glare she hoped would keep her quiet.

Mariska's expression darkened as she offered Stephanie one last scowl. Stephanie stuck her tongue out at her.

Someone pounded on the front door.

"Stay behind the bar," repeated Declan.

"What do you want?" called Seamus in a booming baritone.

"Leave the building and get in your cars and there will be no trouble."

"I've heard that one before," muttered Stephanie.

"You can't kill us all," continued Seamus, ignoring her. "There are a lot of us in here. You can't kill this many people without blowback. One is the wife of a sheriff—"

Declan lunged to slap his hand over his uncle's mouth.

"Are you crazy?" he hissed. His voice dropped lower and Charlotte crept forward to listen, though she'd already realized Seamus's mistake.

"Don't give them leverage," whispered Declan.

Seamus cursed beneath Declan's palm.

"Frank will have the whole department out here!" screamed Darla.

Charlotte whirled waving her hands in the air. "Darla, *no!*"

Darla's brow knit. "What? If they know we're friends with the Sheriff it will scare them away."

Charlotte scurried behind the bar to Darla. "They know we have no way of reaching anyone. They cut the phone lines. But *they* can get to Frank."

"Get to Frank?" Darla took a moment and then gasped, covering her mouth with her hand. "You mean they'll threaten to kill him if we don't come out."

"Sheriff Frank, eh?" said the voice outside.

Charlotte closed her eyes, breath releasing from her body.

CHAPTER NINETEEN

Something on the roof of the disco rattled and all eyes trained upward. The glittery ball hanging in the center of the dance floor shook and began to slowly spin.

"I think you have pigeons," said Stephanie. She grabbed her gun from the bar top and shot once through the ceiling in one fluid movement.

Caught off guard, the ladies behind the bar released a string of yelps.

A second later they heard someone outside call out, a scuffling noise on the roof, and then a loud *Oof!* at the front of the building.

"Did someone fall? Did you get him?" asked Darla.

Stephanie shrugged and set her gun back down.

"Don't start *shooting*," snapped Declan, visibly angry.

Stephanie rolled her eyes. "I've had enough of this." She strode toward the front door. "Pirro! Go away. Let me get rid of these people and you can have the building."

"Hey!" called Jackie.

Seamus held up a hand, asking her to be quiet.

"That you in there, Rubia?" asked Pirro.

Stephanie put a hand on her hip. "*Leave* or I'll kill you all.

How about that? Nice and slow, too."

Darla's eyes bulged. "Would she do that?"

"I told you she was up to no good," muttered Mariska.

Pirro called back. "I don't think so, Rubia. You killed my friend."

"Actually Pirro killed his friend," offered Declan. "If Pirro is the redhead. We saw it on the security cameras."

Stephanie grinned and called outside. "Hey, clown—*you* killed your friend, didn't you?"

There was a pause. "No. *You* killed him."

"There are cameras, moron. We *saw* you kill him."

"He was going to die anyway. I put him out of his pain."

Stephanie glanced at Declan. "He has a point. I get to count that one."

Declan frowned and Stephanie's expression flashed regret, as if she'd been hoping Declan would high-five her for the kill. Charlotte found the exchange curious.

That almost looked like she'd wanted Declan's approval.

Maybe Stephanie still had feelings for Declan after all... She'd always assumed the vicious blonde just had a bad case of wanting what she couldn't have. For the first time, Charlotte felt a little sorry for her.

"You come out or we'll shoot you out," called Pirro, bringing the conversation full circle.

"Do you really want to mess up your boss's building?" asked Stephanie.

There was a pause. "You come out or we'll kill *Sheriff Frank*."

Darla yipped. "What have I done?"

Charlotte's nervous stomach did another flip. Not only were they all already in danger, but she had no way to warn Frank of the trouble headed his way. They were trapped like rats, though rats always seemed to find a way out—

Charlotte paused, picturing rats in a sewer scurrying

through the tunnels.

Something clicked.

Charlotte pulled the map from her pocket and unfolded it on the bar.

"I thought they wanted to build a road here from another facility."

"What's that?" asked Declan, moving towards her.

"This map Jackie found in the parking lot. I realized this loose jumble of boxes actually fits the room pattern of the club."

Declan placed a finger on the map. "You're right. This part is definitely the club. And this is the road?"

"There's no road there now," said Jackie, rising just high enough to peek at the map.

"That's what I thought at first. A road, right? But it isn't a road. The lines are dashed. It's a *tunnel*."

"An existing tunnel?"

"I don't know. But if it is, we can get out of here." Charlotte looked at Jackie, whose expression filled with worry.

"I don't know anything about a tunnel."

Charlotte studied the map. *I have to be right.* The lines that led away from the building—if the dashed-line tube it created was drawn to scale with the rest of the rooms, it wasn't a road or some sort of hamster tube. It was man-sized. And what was a giant, man-sized hamster tube but...*a tunnel.*

"It leads from this side of the building. Is there a basement?"

Jackie snorted a laugh. "In Florida?"

Charlotte nodded. Of course not. Especially not here in the swamp.

"That's a good point," said Declan. "How did they build a tunnel through the swamp?"

Charlotte considered her hamster tube analogy. "Some sort of piping maybe? Oh no...Jackie, you said you reinforced the walls. Did you do the whole building?"

Declan's shoulder's slumped. "Right. She would have found the tunnel if it was there."

Jackie nodded. "We went around the whole building...except..." She turned and stared at the bar shelving. On either side of the giant wooden structure Charlotte could see the walls had been built out by the cement block, effectively embedding the bar in the wall.

Charlotte finished Jackie's sentence. "*Except behind the bar.* Please tell me the bar was here when you bought the club?"

Jackie nodded. "It was. It's why I bought the place. It felt like it was fate."

"Who did you buy it from?"

"Um...some group called Georgette Enterprises."

Stephanie perked. "Georgette Enterprises? That's Louis's mom. His father named one of his companies after her. Louis told me the whole boring story."

"So that's why Louis and Pirro know about the tunnel," said Charlotte.

"Could they take the tunnel to get to us?" asked Declan.

Charlotte stared up at the bar back. "Maybe they could...but there's no point. Even if they have access to the other side, they think it's sealed on this side. *Behind the bar.*"

Charlotte locked eyes with Stephanie and pointed to the front door. "Stall Pirro. Don't let him send people for Frank."

She turned to Jackie.

"Sweetheart, I'm afraid we're going to have to destroy your   bar."

CHAPTER TWENTY

Declan appeared with a hammer in his hand.

"Couldn't find an axe?" asked Charlotte.

"Sadly, no. I spotted this back in the utility room during our check, though."

Jackie stood, seemingly dumbstruck, gaping at the hammer in Declan's hand.

"Do you have a fire axe or something like that here?" he asked.

Jackie continued to stare at the hammer.

"*Jackie.*"

Darla poked at her friend and Jackie jerked back into the present. "What?"

"Declan asked you if you have an axe."

"An axe?"

"Like a lumberjack."

"No. Why would I have an axe?" Jackie looked at Charlotte. "You're not thinking about axing my beautiful bar, are you?"

Charlotte crossed her arms over her chest. "We could stay here and die if you prefer."

"Or they could kidnap and kill Frank," added Darla.

Jackie put her face in her hands. "This is terrible. *Fine.* Do what you have to do but I don't have to watch."

Mariska patted her on the shoulder. "We'll remove all the bottles and glasses first."

Jackie nodded and everyone but Stephanie began clearing the shelves.

"I'm running out of ideas for stalling them," said Stephanie.

Charlotte stared at the ceiling, thinking. "Just make small talk. Do you have shared history you could wax poetic about?"

"Wax poetic? Do I look like Edgar Allan Poe?" Stephanie looked at Declan. "Where did you get this one?"

"Just *talk,*" said Declan.

Stephanie huffed and called to Pirro. "Remember that time you kidnapped Rico's corner thug? Did you cut off his ear or his finger first?"

Pirro laughed. Mariska's eyes grew wide as golf balls. Each time Stephanie recalled another appalling thing Pirro had done, all heads turned to stare at her in horror. Pirro guffawed and gabbed like the standoff was a coffee clutch.

Charlotte suspected Pirro was stalling for time, too, but couldn't work out why.

As soon as the bar shelves were clear of glassware, Seamus hauled back the mallet he'd been impatiently cuddling and started smashing. Wood split in two and exploded from the cabinet. Jackie moaned.

Declan grabbed Seamus's arm before he could swing again. "Shhh."

"What?"

"The shelves pull out. Just remove them. And try not to make so much noise. We don't want Pirro to know what we're up to."

Seamus scowled. "How would he know we're destroying Jackie's bar?"

"We don't know what he knows. He might know about the tunnel. He might be the guy who dropped that map in the first place."

"Hm. Good point, boyo."

They removed the shelves. Charlotte rapped the back of the bar, searching for a likely spot to start bashing.

"Sounds like there's a wall behind this side."

Seamus followed her lead and knocked on the opposite side. "Here too."

Declan tapped on the center. The sound made his expression darken. "This doesn't sound promising either."

"Just hit it," suggested Seamus.

Declan took a deep breath and pulled back his hammer. "Here goes nothing."

Thrusting forward, hammer met wood. The veneer cracked. Charlotte thought she heard something crack and tumble to the ground behind the wall.

She winced. She'd seen the power with which Declan hit the back of the bar, only to be denied. While the wood was cracked, they hadn't made any real progress. Behind her, she could hear Stephanie running out of ways to delay Pirro's wrath.

"Yikes. That didn't go far."

Declan took a few more swings, pausing for different time periods between each strike to keep Pirro from noticing an obvious hammering pattern ringing from inside. After the fourth swing, he put down the tool and clawed at the cracked wood. Wedging his fingers behind a sizable chunk, he peeled it back to reveal red brick.

"I thought you said you didn't have them brick this wall," he said to Jackie.

"They didn't. I had them concrete block everything. I never saw them with bricks."

Declan grimaced. "They must have bricked up the tunnel

before they built the bar in front of it."

Charlotte nodded. "Right. Of course. They never would have been able to sell the place with a giant drug tunnel attached to it."

Declan wiped his brow. "This is slow-going. There must be two layers of brick here."

Charlotte craned her neck to survey the bar. She remembered seeing something that might help. *Columns.* Jackie had some decorative Greek columns stacked in a corner of the dancefloor.

"I have an idea, but I need to know if those columns over there are real."

Jackie followed where Charlotte pointed and nodded. "Yes, they are. They weigh a ton."

"You're thinking we could use them as a battering ram?" asked Seamus.

She nodded. "There isn't a ton of room to get it swinging with the rest of the bar here, but I'm thinking maybe the shorter one?"

Declan and Seamus moved to the dance floor and returned with the shortest column. The two men held the cement column low and after a few practice swings, pounded the wall as hard as they could. Charlotte heard some of the internal bricks fall to the ground, and soon they had a hole big enough for even the broadest of them to fit through.

"What are you doing in there?" roared Pirro from outside.

"We're bored. Decided to redecorate," returned Stephanie.

"Flashlight, hurry," said Declan.

Jackie ran into her office and appeared with a large LED flashlight. Everyone in Florida always had a good-sized flashlight handy. Electric lines and Florida storms constantly wrestled for the belt.

Declan pointed the light into the tunnel, only to find another brick wall stood four feet into the hole.

"You've got to be kidding me," mumbled Declan.

"We're going to die," said Mariska.

"Wait—" Declan dropped the beam downward. "There's a ladder here. It's like we're at the top of a manhole."

"Right, we're too high here. The tunnel has to be below the foundation."

"But you said that's impossible in Florida," said Darla.

Declan crawled through the hole they'd created and climbed down the ladder.

"It's a giant pipeline down here," he called back to the group.

"All good?" asked Seamus, his head stuck through the hole in the wall.

There was a pause. "Looks good. Start moving people."

Seamus helped Darla, Jackie and Mariska through the hole.

A loud crashing sound echoed from the front of the building. Apparently, Pirro and his men had decided they'd waited long enough to break down the door. Charlotte could see the building shake with every crash. Whatever they were using as a battering ram, it was more effective than Seamus's rubber mallet. Charlotte suspected it was a vehicle they'd been waiting to arrive. This reinforced her hunch—Pirro had needed to delay as much as they did.

"You're next," said Seamus to Charlotte.

Declan called up the ladder. "Seamus—get Stephanie's gun. We'll need protection front and back."

Seamus looked at Stephanie.

"Good luck with that," she said, gun in hand.

"You want to protect the back?" asked Charlotte.

Stephanie opened the revolver, counted her remaining bullets and slammed it closed. "I'll stay here."

Charlotte scowled. "You couldn't have more than five bullets in there."

"Four."

"They're going to kill you."

Stephanie shook her head. "Pirro wouldn't dare."

"We can't just leave you here."

Stephanie smiled. "Just go, Susie Sunshine."

Charlotte looked to Seamus, but he only shrugged and ushered her to the tunnel. With one last glance back at Stephanie, she stepped through the hole, turning to negotiate the ladder. She needed to concentrate on keeping her footing, but her mind swirled with the endless possibilities awaiting them at the end of the tunnel.

What if the other side was bricked off as well? We'd be sitting ducks in a tunnel.

Nothing about their plan seemed certain.

There was another crash at the front door.

Time to move.

Charlotte climbed down the ladder. At the bottom she saw the others huddling inside what appeared to be a long metal tube, empty and smooth but for where the lip of one section met the next.

Declan held up his gun for Charlotte to see. "I'm going to lead the way for now."

Seamus climbed down.

"Do you have the gun?" asked Declan.

"Procuring madam's weapon was easier said than done."

"Is she coming?"

"She is not."

"We can't leave her up there."

"She says they can't kill her."

"Why?"

Seamus shrugged.

Even in the dim light Charlotte could see Declan wasn't happy. Another crash echoed from above.

"Okay. We don't have time. Let's go. Watch the back

Seamus. First sign of anything let me know."

Declan squeezed past the ladies and led the way.

CHAPTER TWENTY-ONE

They hustled through the alien landscape of metal tubing for ten minutes before Declan motioned for them to stop. From the back of the pack, Charlotte could see his flashlight rise into the air and illuminate bars protruding from the wall. He'd found another ladder.

They clustered close as Declan mounted the rungs, flashlight beneath his arm. He struggled to open the hatch.

"I'll hold the light on it," suggested Charlotte.

He handed down the flashlight and she directed the beam on the hatch, revealing a metal pin on a chain tucked along the edge. Declan removed it to release the lock. The hatch swung up and open. Sunlight flooded into the tunnel, the group collectively shielding their eyes from the glare.

Declan pulled his phone from his pocket and attempted a call. A moment later he descended again.

"Swamp. I think we're better off continuing through the tunnel."

"No signal?" asked Darla, though they all knew his response.

"Nothing yet. I suspect these escape hatches are scattered along the way. Emergency escape routes."

"Isn't it safer out of this pipe?" asked Jackie.

Declan shook his head. "You know the hellish bogs the news shows in the background whenever they run a story about the guys hunting pythons in the swamp?"

Mariska grimaced. "Gotcha. Think I'll take my chances in here."

"Isn't disappearing into the muck better than being mowed down by druggies?" asked Jackie.

"I think *druggies* are the people who take the drugs, not the people who sell them," said Mariska.

Jackie's eyes grew wild. "You know what I mean!"

Seamus moved to put his arm around his girlfriend. Charlotte didn't need the glow of Declan's flashlight to see Jackie had run out of coping mechanisms. The woman was having a monumentally bad day.

Declan did his best to move past the tension. "It's too dangerous out there. Too easy to get lost. Let's hope the next exit has a path to civilization."

"And a phone signal," muttered Darla.

They continued their hurried walk down the pipeline. A few steps into their travels, Charlotte did an about-face and jogged back to the ladder. In the dying glow of the far-off flashlight, she peered at the hatch deep in thought.

"Don't dally," called Seamus, comforting a now sobbing Jackie at the back of the pack.

"Just taking a quick peek. I'm right behind you."

She climbed the ladder and opened the hatch. As soon as her eyes adjusted to the light, she knew Declan hadn't been exaggerating. They wouldn't last two minutes in the swampland surrounding this exit.

She was about to descend when gunfire erupted to her left.

Pirro's men had breached the disco's door.

It wouldn't be long before armed men came running

down the tunnel. Even if Stephanie could negotiate *her* release, she probably didn't have the pull to change *all* the thugs' plans. They were still in danger.

To her right, she heard the group yelp with fear and break into a panicked trot.

A final few pops of gunfire echoed from the direction of the disco.

Had they not spared Stephanie?

Without knowing what lay ahead of them, the others would be sitting ducks once Pirro and his men made progress down the tunnel. The ladies weren't speedy joggers.

I have to do something. Think.

Charlotte's gaze rose to the hatch.

It's a longshot...

Scurrying up the ladder, Charlotte hauled herself into the swamp. The mud squished around her flip flops, claiming them as its own the moment she tried to walk.

Balancing the hatch open she decided the easiest direction in which to travel. It seemed more wet to the west. The east had more trees.

West it is.

She mucked her way through the worst of the mud, taking a multitude of steps, back and forth along her own trail, until it appeared a large group had made their way in that direction. She broke every branch and smooshed every reed she could find. She retrieved and tossed her flip flops in that direction.

Returning to the hatch a final time, she stuck her head inside. Voices. She could hear men coming.

There wasn't any time to lose.

She worked her way east to the trees, covering her tracks with her toes and hands as she went, like a baker smoothing the icing on a cake. The mud seemed eager to help her, swallowing every footprint with the smallest provocation.

Reaching a large, lonely cypress, she ran to its opposite side and put her back against it, panting.

"It's like a swamp," said a voice a moment later.

Charlotte caught her breath and then almost immediately had to continue panting quietly through her nose. Her lungs burned.

I really have to work on my stamina.

She peered around the tree and spotted a head sticking from the ground. Pirro's men had arrived.

There was another voice, muffled. She couldn't make out what the other person said, but the man above ground replied, "Yeah, I can see the way they went but it's nasty out here, Pirro."

Looking miserable, the man climbed from the hole. Two others joined him, including the one with the strange red hair Charlotte had watched shoot his friend.

She could hear her own heartbeat, banging in her ears. She couldn't believe the men couldn't hear it.

She peeked again as the men headed west through the muck. One of them rattled off something in Spanish but she only recognized the curse words. They gave her a general idea of the speaker's frame of mind.

They were pissed.

Charlotte pressed her spine against the tree. Something mosquito-y bit her shoulder and she slapped at it without thinking.

"Ow!"

Oh no.

She froze, wondering how loud she'd been.

The mucking noise of the men's shoes being swallowed by the mud stopped.

Squatting, she peered around the tree, hoping if they were looking in her direction, they wouldn't be looking that low.

Six eyes trained on her from the far side of the marsh.

"There!" yelled one, pointing.

Whoops.

The men hollered and launched into a flurry of action, arms flailing, knees rising, hampered by the depth of the mud, sloppily running towards her.

Everything in Charlotte's body told her to bolt *away* from them.

Her mind said, 'no.'

Her mind said, 'Get in the hole.'

Stupid mind.

It isn't easy listening to a brain when the rest of the body is screaming for an opposing idea. And it isn't easy getting a body to do something it doesn't want to do. But a moment later, Charlotte found herself sprinting *toward* the men.

They were so stunned they stopped for a moment.

Then they realized she had no weapon.

She was just closer to the open hatch than they were.

Releasing another string of profanities in at least two different languages, they began slopping forward again.

The lead man wrestled to pull a pistol from the waistline of his baggy jeans.

Guns. I forgot about the guns. How did I forget about the guns?

Charlotte faltered. There was nowhere to hide from bullets.

The lead man tripped and fell forward to his knees, sinking his gun deep into the mud as the men behind him fell over him, scrambling to get around their fallen comrade. They hadn't yet pulled their guns, but now they grabbed for them.

Charlotte silently thanked the lead man's wet jeans for dragging him into the mud and planting his gun where it couldn't hurt her.

She dove for the hatch as the first usable gun fired.

Sliding like a baseball player through the mud and reeds, she grabbed the edge of the hatch to stop her momentum and swung her legs into the hole. Her instincts told her to skip the ladder and drop to the floor but she knew she had to lock the hatch. As she fell, she grabbed a ladder rung and hung, suspended in mid-air for a moment.

Her wet fingers began to slide off the rung.

Flailing, she found another rung with her feet and grabbed the hatch with her free hand. The men were three feet from her now.

She slammed it shut.

Please, Please let me find the lock.

She'd forgotten closing the hatch would plunge her into total darkness. Panic rose in her chest as her fingers searched for the bolt that would seal the clip.

She'd had to release the bolt to open the hatch on the way out and knew it was hanging from a chain. It banged against her fingers, taunting her. Someone slammed against the hatch. In a moment they would jerk it open, wrenching it from her hands...*and probably shoot her in the head.*

Another tap on her fingertip by the bolt and then—

Got it.

Her digits encircled the bolt and she slammed it into place. She didn't know how she found the slot so fast. She imagined the feeling was akin to Luke Skywalker watching his bomb shoot through the Death Star's thermal exhaust port.

The hatch rattled as someone yanked it. Out in the swamp, the cursing began in earnest.

Charlotte felt her way down the ladder, slipping when a gunshot exploded above her, followed by what sounded like the ringing of a bell. She fell to the ground and covered her head, curled in the fetal position.

Someone screamed. More cursing.

The bullet hadn't penetrated. If she had to guess, it had

ricocheted and hit someone.

A beam of light struck her body, and she jerked, covering her head again, sure the hatch had opened.

They must have found a way to shoot the lock. Stupid idea—

"Charlotte!"

She peered from beneath her arms. Declan ran towards her, flashlight in hand. He knelt beside her.

Dirty and half-covered in shadows, he had never been so gorgeous.

"Are you okay? What happened? Seamus said you were right behind him and then you weren't."

Charlotte uncurled and sat up, her hand still on her beating heart. "I'm fine. We should get out from beneath the hatch though, just in case."

More muffled screaming echoed from above. Someone screamed *Freedom!* at the top of their lungs. Declan stared up at the rattling hatch.

"Who is that and why does he sound like the end of *Braveheart?*"

"It's Pirro and his men. They breeched Jackie's. I heard gunfire and knew they were coming. So I made it look like we went up there."

"And they followed you?"

She nodded. "I led them one way and hid the other. When they followed what they thought were my tracks I ran back to the hatch and closed it."

Declan's mouth gaped. "That was *insane*. You could have been killed."

"We would've all been killed if they came down the tunnel."

Declan scooped her up in his arms and pressed her against his chest.

"Charlotte. They have *guns*. You can't do things like that."

"Sorry," she mumbled, her lips pressed against his neck.

He smelled good. Maybe anything smelled good after the methane stench of the swamp.

When he released her she found her eyes had watered either from relief or adrenalin. She sniffed and took a deep, calming breath. "Where are the others?"

"There was a door at the other end that led into a little diner in the middle of nowhere. We opened it and found ourselves staring at empty orange crates."

"A friendly diner?"

"Seems to be. I guess Louis hadn't made a move on them yet. They let us call the police."

Above, the rattling had stopped.

"They quit trying to get in," said Charlotte.

Declan helped her to her feet. "That means they're probably on their way back to Jackie's or the diner, if they know about it."

Charlotte gasped. "*Stephanie.* Did you call an ambulance?"

He nodded. "I'm sure there are police on their way there as well."

"Stephanie's still there."

"I'm sure she's long gone. She'll have talked her way out—"

Charlotte shook her head. "I don't think so. I heard gunfire."

Declan frowned. "You follow the tunnel to the diner. The cops will be there any second. I'll go check on Stephanie."

Charlotte grabbed a ladder rung to pull herself to her feet. "No way. I'm coming. Let's go."

Declan opened his mouth to argue.

"I'm *coming*," she repeated, before he could speak.

Declan pointed to the ceiling. "It won't take those men long to get back to the disco."

"Yes it will. It's all swamp up there. It will take them *forever* to slog back, assuming they're not eaten by an alligator or a python. We can *run*. The cops will be at Jackie's by the time those men get close."

"What if they left men back at the club?"

Charlotte considered this. "I'll let you and your gun go in first."

Declan sighed. "Fine. But stay behind me."

"Because you're a big bad soldier?"

"Because I know I'll never talk you out of going."

CHAPTER TWENTY-TWO

Declan poked his head through the wall into Jackie's bar. Clinging precariously on the ladder behind him, Charlotte strained to get a view of her own.

Declan glanced back at her. "Do you really need to be *right* behind me? I feel like I'm carrying you up the ladder on my back."

"Like a fireman."

"A fireman who carries people *into* the fire?"

Charlotte knew he had a point so she changed the subject. "I don't hear anything."

"Me neither. Un-Velcro yourself from my legs and hang back a second."

He pulled himself up and climbed through the hole in the wall.

One Mississippi...

Charlotte followed.

Declan crept around the bar, staying low, his gun raised. Now inside, Charlotte could hear a strange, rhythmic wheezing noise.

"What is that?" she whispered.

Declan turned and raised his finger to his lips.

They crept a few more paces forward. The front door of the Disco had been obliterated by something. Presumably, the small pickup truck parked on the threshold. The driver-side door hung open and a man lay on the ground beneath it, unmoving.

As they rounded the bar, a grunting erupted to their right. Declan whipped his gun in the direction of the noise. It was the man who'd first attacked them, still tied to the bar. He must have awakened during all the commotion and now strained against his bindings. He turned, spotting them.

"Let me go!" he roared.

A movement close to the center of the dance floor caught Charlotte's eye.

Stephanie.

She lay on her back, arm reaching toward them.

Declan glanced once more at the man tied to the bar and ran to Stephanie. Charlotte followed, giving the angry man wide berth as he kicked at her.

Stephanie breathed in short, shallow breaths.

"'Bout time," she whispered.

A growing red stain marred the front of her shirt. Declan tore it open to find the wound.

Stephanie winced as the fabric ripped. "Burberry."

"It was stained anyway, there was no way that was going to come out," said Charlotte, unsure why she felt compelled to make Stephanie feel better about her expensive shirt. Probably, she reasoned, because it would be more difficult to make her feel good about the hole in her chest. It bubbled when Stephanie breathed, little blood spheres growing and popping.

That can't be good.

Declan frowned. "Her lung collapsed. I need tape. Where did I leave that first aid kit we used to cover your shoulder?

Charlotte squinted, thinking. "Should still be in the

kitchen?"

"Okay. Hold your hand over that hole—"

"—we don't want air getting into the chest cavity," said Declan and Charlotte in unison.

They looked at each other.

"How do you know that?" asked Charlotte.

"I was trained to treat field wounds like this. How do *you* know that?"

"I saw it on television."

"*Adorable*," wheezed Stephanie. Her eyes locked with Declan's and rocked back and forth as if she was using them to point. They both followed her direction and spotted a gun on the ground a few feet away.

Declan nodded. "I'll be right back with bandages." He stood, snatching the gun from the ground on his way to search for medical supplies.

Charlotte watched him go. She had so many questions. Did he pick up the gun because Stephanie used it to kill the man in the truck? She wasn't sure covering for Stephanie was the right move, but the crazy blonde *had* stayed behind to cover them as they made their escape—

"Hole."

Charlotte snapped from her thoughts and found Stephanie staring at her.

"Sorry." She covered the bubbling hole with Stephanie's shirt and pressed lightly down on it. Stephanie moaned, her eyes screwed tightly shut.

"That's a really pretty bra," said Charlotte, wondering how to make small talk when plugging a woman's lung hole like a little Dutch boy with his finger in the dyke. "Thanks for staying back here. You really didn't have to."

"Now...you tell me," said Stephanie between gasps for air. She kept her eyes closed. Outside, Charlotte heard sirens. Stephanie heard them as well, eyes popping wide.

Charlotte glanced through the destroyed front door. "That's the ambulance. We called one. Well, Declan did. I was tricking Pirro and his men into getting lost in the swamp. But, yeah. Ambulance. We forgot to tell you there was one coming."

Stephanie glared at her.

Charlotte smiled, counting the seconds until the EMTs arrived. Less for Stephanie's discomfort and more for hers.

CHAPTER TWENTY-THREE

Dallas held up the playing cards for Ryan to consider using his one good eye. Dallas had long ago tired of beating the older man. Instead, he'd shifted to beating his own boredom by playing five card draw poker with his prisoner.

For comfort, the reedy henchman had agreed to bind Ryan's hands to the chair arms instead of zip-tying them behind his back. The solution left Ryan still unable to hold his cards, so Dallas splayed the cards like a fan, backs to himself, following each deal.

Ryan considered his hand. "I'll keep the second, fourth and fifth. Left to right."

"Your left or my left?"

"Same as last time. My left to right."

Dallas took a moment to do the calculations, lips moving like a child learning to read. For the life of him, Ryan couldn't imagine what directional computations the boy employed deciding *right* from *left*.

Dallas plucked the cards from Ryan's hand and pulled two new ones. The boy couldn't stop grinning. He was the worst poker player Ryan had ever seen.

"Gotta good hand, so you—"

Outside the room, the squawk of a walkie-talkie broke the silence.

Ryan and Dallas froze, staring at each other.

"What was that?" whispered Dallas.

Ryan shrugged. "This is *your* place."

The radio quacked again. *"43. 10-14 at Elm and Constitution."*

Dallas's bulging eyes looked like fried eggs with dull brown yolks floating in the center.

"43. 10-6," replied a man's voice.

Dallas gasped. "It's a cop."

Ryan nodded, straining his neck to catch a better view of their little room. In the corner stood what he guessed was a closet.

"Untie me. We can hide in that closet."

Dallas grimaced. "Won't they look in the closet?"

"I'm not sure, but they'll *definitely* look in the room."

Dallas jumped to his feet and thrust his hand in his pocket. Flipping out a switchblade, he cut the cords around Ryan's left wrist with one deft movement.

Ryan was impressed. What the boy lacked in brains, he made up for in agility.

"Hide the card game. Try to make it look like no one is here."

Dallas looked at the splatter on the ground with dismay. "What about the blood?"

"Do your best." Ryan grabbed the bloody towel Dallas had used to clean his face when they shifted from fists to cards and headed for the closet. Opening the door, he found the space empty but for some clothes on hangers.

"43. Uh...10-22. It's her husband wearing some kind of pirate costume..."

Ryan had listened to enough police scanners since his son's death to know the cop would soon enter the room.

Dispatch had asked for the officer's assistance with a pirate prowler, and then cancelled.

Typical day in Florida.

"Hurry," Ryan prodded Dallas.

"43. 10-4," said the cop.

Dallas bolted for the closet and shut the door behind them. They huddled together, noses nearly touching, pressed into a sea of cheap collared shirts.

The door of the room opened.

Dallas held his breath, much to Ryan's relief. The boy smelled like tobacco chew and spiced-meat sticks.

A few moments later, the click of a door shutting told them the officer had seen enough and left.

"I think he's gone," whispered Dallas.

"Give it a second."

"Hey... Why didn't you yell out?"

"Hm?"

"Why did you hide? You could have yelled for the cop and gotten away."

Ryan cracked open the door to the closet and peeked out. The room was empty. The outer door was closed.

He walked to the exit and put his ear against the door, hearing only the hum of machinery.

"I think we're good."

Dallas had followed him halfway to the door and stood staring at him, hands on hips.

"Seriously, dude. Why didn't you try to get away?"

Ryan smiled, lifting the blood-covered white towel in his hand to reveal the gun he held beneath it. In the panic to hide the evidence, Dallas had forgotten he'd placed his gun on the table. Ryan had carried it into the closet.

"For the same reason I didn't shoot you."

For the second time in ten minutes, Dallas's eyes saucered. He raised his hands. "Easy buddy. No hard feelings.

I've just been doin' my job—"

"You have to tell me these things—" The door behind Ryan burst open and he stumbled back to avoid being knocked over.

"*Louis,*" said Dallas.

Ryan could tell the boy didn't know if he should be relieved or horrified. His gaze shot to the gun in Ryan's hand. Ryan lowered the weapon and let the towel drop over it.

Louis turned his palms to the air and addressed Dallas. "So *now*—after I let a cop in because I thought I had nothing to hide—Johnny tells me you've been asking to see me about some prisoner you've got stashed in here?"

Dallas nodded and glanced at Ryan.

Louis followed his gaze and turned, wincing upon spotting Ryan's face.

"What happened to the one side of your face? You look like Two-Face, the Batman guy."

"Kid's a lefty," said Ryan.

Louis lifted his hands in the air and let them fall against his thighs with a slap. "What's going on here?"

Dallas swallowed. "We heard the cop coming and hid in the closet. But—"

Louis cut him short. "Oh, good job. But...how'd you keep *him* quiet? And why is he standing there like he works for me?"

Ryan cleared his throat. "Because I do want to work for you."

"Boss—" Dallas tried again.

"What?" Louis looked from Dallas to Ryan and back again for explanation. "Who *is* this guy?"

Dallas scratched his head. "He was watching us. We brought him here to find out why, but you need to know—"

"Who said to bring him to my dry cleaning?"

"Pirro said you wanted us to grab him and find out what

he's up to."

"I never—" Louis cleared his throat. "Oh, right. I forgot. So, what'd he say?"

"He wouldn't talk to anyone but the boss, even when I roughed him up."

"The boss? That's *me*," said Louis. He grinned at Ryan as if he'd just won a trophy.

"You're the *big* boss?" clarified Ryan.

Louis' smile dropped. He seemed unsure. "Yes..."

"You'd be the one to talk to about the books?"

"What books?"

"Clothes aren't the only things you need to launder, right? Thanks to your other business?"

"Uh..."

Ryan decided not to wait for Louis to ask *what other business?* "Louis—if I can call you Louis—I'm an expert at hiding money. Money that maybe didn't derive from a legal enterprise."

Louis appeared trapped somewhere between confused and angry. He shot his attention back to Dallas. "Is that what he told you?"

"That's just it, boss. He wouldn't tell me anything. He said he'd only talk to you. But—"

"So why didn't you call me?"

"I *did*. I told Johnny to get you like six times. Thing is—"

"I just saw Johnny. He didn't say a word until after the cops came in and left."

Dallas shrugged, shaking his head. "I tol' him."

"He did. I was here," offered Ryan. He didn't know who Johnny was in the grand scheme of things, but he'd seen Dallas ask the man to get Louis earlier. For whatever reason, Johnny had ignored the boy.

Louis turned back to Ryan. "So you were following my men in the hopes of talking to me?"

Ryan nodded.

Louis thrust his hands into his pockets, staring at the ground in silence for some time.

"I'll be honest with you. The books have been a problem. There seems to be a lot of money missing, but Pirro says—" He scowled. "Wait. How do I know I can trust you?"

"He's got a gun," spat Dallas, as if the phrase had been building up inside him for some time.

"*What?*"

Ryan lifted the towel to reveal the gun. Louis leapt behind Dallas and hissed in the boy's ear. "Why didn't you tell me?"

"I tried to!"

Ryan put the gun on the cardboard box they'd been using as a makeshift card table and stepped away from it.

"I'm not here to shoot you. I told you, I want to work for you. Why would I have hidden from the police if I wanted to get away?"

Louis pondered this for a few seconds. "Oh—*I know*— what if you *are* a cop?"

"Ooh, good one, Louis," said Dallas.

Louis glared at him.

Dallas cleared his throat. "I mean, *Mr. Beaumont.*"

Ryan raised a palm. "Take a few days. Look into me. I'm not a cop."

"And that's why you were following my men? To help me with my books?"

Ryan nodded.

Louis appeared to consider this. "If I showed you my spreadsheets, could you tell if someone was robbing me?"

"Sure."

"Would you do it, like, as a test of your skills?"

"You mean on spec? Sure."

Louis stared at him until Ryan felt the man was waiting for him to hop into action.

"You want me to look at them now?"

"Huh? Oh. No. I guess you'd probably like to clean up or something. Your face—"

"It would be nice to see through two eyes. Maybe get a shower and put some ice on this..."

"Right. Okay. I guess you can go home. Maybe you can come back tomorrow and I'll walk you through things?"

"Sounds good." Ryan remained still until Louis grew visibly uncomfortable.

"Why are you looking at me like that?"

Ryan snapped from his thoughts. "Sorry. I—"

"What?"

"Nothing."

Ryan left the room and headed toward daylight at the front of the shop. Men and women working the dry cleaning machines glanced at him and returned to their business.

Ryan couldn't shake his disappointment.

He thought for sure Louis would be a redhead.

CHAPTER TWENTY-FOUR

Charlotte sat at Mariska's counter drinking coffee. She'd wandered over to make sure Mariska was okay after the ordeal at Jackie's club.

Mariska seemed normal. She couldn't stop talking about food.

"That was the worst diner on the planet. Nothing. Not a single bagel. Not even pie."

Charlotte chuckled. "I'm sure it was better than a metal pipeline under the swamp."

Mariska rolled her eyes. "*Barely*. I was thirsty after all that and they didn't have any orange juice to help with my blood sugar."

"They didn't have any food at all?"

"Coffee. But who wants coffee when you're really thirsty?"

"Maybe they weren't open yet."

"There were two men sitting there drinking coffee when we came in. They just about had heart attacks when we all came spilling out of the back room."

"Maybe they weren't customers. Was there a waitress or a cook?"

Mariska scowled. "Now that you mention it—no. Those two men drinking their coffee were the only people there."

Charlotte shrugged. "See? They weren't open. They were probably workers."

Mariska nodded. "They looked like workers. They had stuff all over their arms." She danced her finger over her forearms, which Charlotte knew as Mariska's sign for *tattoos*.

Darla walked in with Frank on her heels.

Charlotte was thrilled to see Frank. After being questioned by police following their tunnel escape, Charlotte had discovered very little about the police investigation into the attack on Jackie's disco. They'd been separated from each other for questioning, so she hadn't had a chance to compare notes. A late-night call to Declan had gone unanswered. It had been less than twenty-four hours, but she needed to start clearing her plate.

The first thing she'd done upon waking was call Frank and ask him to glean all the information he could from the police who'd handled the disco scene.

"Did you call them?" asked Charlotte.

Sheriff Frank took his hat off as he rambled to the counter. "What a mess that was."

"Is everything sorted out? Did they find the guys in the swamp?"

"I hope they drowned," grumbled Darla, getting herself a cup of coffee.

Frank dropped into a seat and leaned back, the old chair tilting precariously to the right.

"No swamp men."

Charlotte gasped. "None? They got away?"

Frank nodded. "I don't know how much effort went into slopping around the Everglades looking for them, but yes, they got away."

"The Everglades are south of here. That's just swamp

here."

Darla chuckled. "You always were like a little Encyclopedia Britannica."

Charlotte smiled at both the compliment and the fact that few people on the planet even knew what the Encyclopedia Britannica was anymore. That was a bit of history that still lived in Pineapple Port.

"And no sign of the rival gang," added Frank.

Charlotte tucked her head back a notch. "What rival gang?"

"That Stephanie girl told the police a rival gang showed up after you left. They killed that man at the door. Heck of a shot. Right between the eyes."

Charlotte scowled. There had been no rival drug gang. Stephanie needed someone on which to blame the dead men. Someone other than herself. Stephanie shot the man at the door and took a bullet in return, of that she was certain.

I watched Declan take her gun.

But who would believe a pretty, *wounded* attorney shot the man in the doorway *and* the man lying in the parking lot?

"Stephanie said another gang showed up?"

"Yeah, well, she *guessed* they were a rival gang. She doesn't know for sure, of course."

"Of course. How could she?" Charlotte wondered if Frank could hear the sarcasm in her voice. He plowed ahead, apparently oblivious.

"That friend of yours is going to be in the paper for her bravery."

Charlotte straightened. "What? Who? *Stephanie?*"

Frank nodded. "I've had reporters calling all morning trying to reach her. Want to ask her if she was scared, staying behind to protect the rest of you while you escaped. She might have saved you and Darla."

"I still don't trust that girl," mumbled Mariska.

Charlotte felt her mood darken. *She'd* been the one who tricked the bad guys into the swamp. Stephanie stayed behind because she thought she could talk her way out. She didn't want to get picked off with the rest of them in the tunnel. That was the opposite of bravery.

"You heard about how I tricked those guys into the swamp, right?" she asked.

Frank stood to get himself some coffee. "What's that?"

Charlotte slumped in her chair. There were so many stories circulating she didn't want to provide any more information until she could keep things straight. The more they all talked, the more likely they'd end up in trouble. She was starting to feel guilty of something and wasn't sure why.

Watching Declan take that gun makes me an accessory to something, doesn't it?

She sighed. "Never mind."

Frank held up his index finger. "Oh, and we got confirmation that the guy you tied to the bar was definitely mixed up in the drug trade."

"Mm." Charlotte's gaze fell to the floor, musing what that man had seen after the truck crashing through the front door and gunfire awoke him. He could have seen everything. Either way, he probably wasn't saying much.

Probably for the best.

Like a little girl, she wanted to confess everything to Frank, sit back, and wait for him to make everything better. Too bad she was no little girl confessing to accidentally breaking a vase anymore. *She* had unexplained murders and drug lord attacks needing sorting. *She* had to help Jackie unravel herself from the men who wanted her club. *She* had to grill Declan about his past with the Honey Badgers and his future with the gun that killed the man in the disco's doorway. *She* had to find out if Ryan Finnegan was being held by Louis like Stephanie suggested or if he was already dead—

Ryan. I nearly forgot.

"Frank—I told the police I'd overheard something about that Ryan Finnegan I told you about."

"The guy whose condo you broke into?"

"That's the one. I told them I'd overheard he was being held by Louis Beaumont. Did they look into that?" She left out the part about it being Stephanie who told her.

Frank nodded. "That Louis Beaumont—turns out his dad used to be big in the drug trade."

"Did they look for Ryan at his dry cleaners?"

"They did, apparently. Went over there last night and he let them right in the front door. They didn't find anything. He seems legit. Family's not involved in drugs anymore."

"Did the cops go to Ryan's condo? I told them about the condo and the signs of struggle."

Frank shrugged. "I don't know. They had their hands full with Jackie's place. You might want to check in with them if you still think this Ryan fellow's missing."

She nodded. "I'll follow up."

Frank sat again. "Now, if you're finished peppering me with questions, I need to drink my coffee."

"Yep. I should probably go check on Jackie."

Mariska nodded. "That'd be nice. Tell her we all hope she's feeling better and we're sorry about her disco."

"Tell her I'm working with the Tampa P.D. to see what we can figure out for her. I assume her insurance will cover the damage," added Frank.

Charlotte said her goodbyes and borrowed Mariska's car keys.

She already knew her visit to Jackie would wait a little longer.

She needed to talk to Stephanie to clarify what she knew about Ryan before he showed up dead.

And, she needed to talk to Declan.

She tried her boyfriend on her cell as she walked to Mariska's car. Again his phone went to voicemail.

That does it.

She drove directly to Declan's house. Seamus's jalopy sat on the curb outside, but Declan's car was absent from its usual spot in the driveway.

"Where is he?"

Charlotte pushed through Declan's front door and found Seamus on the sofa in his boxers with a beer resting on his thigh. His head swiveled in her direction.

"Jaysus, woman. Have you ever heard of knockin'?"

"Your nephew the drug war soldier. Where is he?"

Seamus stared.

There's something I haven't seen before. Seamus speechless.

After a moment, the Irishman sniffed. "He told you about that, did he?"

"Yes. Right after he beat up a thug like he was Bruce Lee."

Seamus laughed. "Declan has a real talent for that kung fu stuff."

Charlotte felt the corner of her mouth curling into a smile as she recalled the fight.

It was kind of cool.

She forced a frown. *No. Stop it. This is serious.*

"Is he here?"

"He isn't. Wasn't here when I woke up."

Charlotte sighed and sat on the chair opposite Seamus, who held aloft his beer can.

"You want a beer?"

"Little early, don't you think?"

"It's middle of the afternoon in Ireland."

"You haven't been in Ireland for decades. I don't think you're still on Ireland time."

"You'd be surprised."

Seamus stood and disappeared in the back of the house

before reemerging wearing shorts and a t-shirt. He walked to the refrigerator and returned with another beer.

"I'll be honest. My nerves are a bit shot after yesterday," he said.

"Have you talked to Jackie?"

"She went to her sister's. I offered to stay with her but she was scared to sleep in her own house. I'm lettin' her sleep in before I call today."

Charlotte tapped her fingernails to her teeth. She suspected everyone involved in the previous day's attack was a nervous wreck. She definitely didn't feel normal.

"So tell me. You hooked Declan up with The Honey Badgers? You didn't know they were basically mercenaries?"

Seamus chewed on his lip. "I'm not entirely sure what I'm supposed to share at this juncture."

"But that part is true?"

"I'm sure whatever Declan's told you is true. He doesn't like to lie. Especially to you." Seamus took a sip of his beer and squinted at her. "Didn't you know on some level?"

"Know what?"

"Didn't you ever wonder why he looks like he does? Why he swims like he's trying to escape a hungry shark every day in that crazy jet pool of his?"

Charlotte's gaze drifted to the swim-stream pool in Declan's backyard.

Declan is in some insane shape...

"I should have gleaned from his physique he'd been some kind of private soldier?"

Seamus shrugged. "Normal people don't look like that."

Charlotte scowled. "Wait, are you saying he's *still* in the business?"

"No. I—"

Charlotte's phone rang and she scrambled to pull it from her pocket.

It wasn't Declan. It was Gloria.

She stood and held up a finger to ask Seamus to wait.

"Hi Gloria."

"You didn't call yesterday."

Charlotte couldn't help but smile. "You could say I had a busy day yesterday. It was impossible for me to get a moment."

"Have you found anything?"

"I have. Your man's name is Ryan Finnegan."

Gloria repeated the name back to her. "That's a nice name."

"Sure."

"Do you know where he is? *Is he married?*"

Gloria's tone shifted from *concern* to *burning fury* so quickly Charlotte nearly dropped the phone for fear it was hot. "No. I mean, it doesn't look like he's married. He has other issues right now."

"What issues?"

"My only lead thinks he might have been kidnapped by a drug dealer."

"A drug dealer? He's a drug dealer?"

"No—I mean, *again*, I don't think so. I think he's tangled up with one for some reason. I have it on fairly good authority he's being *held* by a drug dealer."

"But why?"

"I don't know."

"Is he in trouble? Did you call the police?"

"I did. I told the police but they haven't found any sign of him."

"What's the drug dealer's name?"

"Louis Beaumont."

"Wha—Georgette's son?"

Charlotte's mind whirred. *Does Gloria know the family? And why does that name sound familiar?*

Georgette Enterprises.

Jackie bought her club from Georgette Enterprises, the company named after Louis's mother.

"Yes. I think Louis's mother is named Georgette. Do you know him?"

"I know *her*."

"How?"

Gloria ignored the question. "Where is he being held?"

"I don't know he's being held at *all*, but someone claimed to see him tied up at a dry cleaners owned by Louis—"

"I have to go. Call me if you find out anything else."

The line went dead.

Charlotte stared at her phone. "Okay then..."

She returned her attention to Seamus hoping to get back to the conversation about Declan possibly *still* working as a mercenary.

Before she could form her next question, the front door opened and Declan entered.

"There's the man of the hour," said Seamus.

Charlotte crossed her arms against her chest. "There you are. I was starting to worry."

Declan grimaced. "Sorry. I went to the hospital to talk to Stephanie."

"She's okay?"

"Made it through surgery with flying colors."

"Good." An uncomfortable silence fell and Charlotte struggled not to say what was on her mind. She lost.

"Did you go to see how she was or to make sure your stories about her gun were straight?"

Charlotte could hear the anger in her own voice. She'd meant it as a straightforward question, but apparently she harbored a little more pique than she'd realized.

"Uh oh," mumbled Seamus. "I think I'm going to go out for a bit."

CHAPTER TWENTY-FIVE

Gloria hung up the phone and stared at it, snipping bits of skin from the inside of her lip with her front teeth.

Georgette Beaumont.

Donning and stripping three different blouses, Gloria settled on one splattered with a swirl of black, white and hot pink paired with a matching hot pink skort. She still had nice legs.

Hopping into her Mercedes, she drove a mile to Seaside Serenade, an assisted-living home not far from her own age-restricted condo. Seaside Serenade was the next step, a step she hoped to avoid for a long time—but it was good to have options. She'd already secured a place for the future, largely on the recommendation of her old friend.

Georgette Beaumont.

A handsome woman with delicate features and dark hair piled high on her head looked up as Gloria entered the Seaside Serenade common room.

The woman's eyes lit with apparent recognition, even as her expression bunched.

"Gloria, what are you doing here? Eez it Tuesday already? I really am losing my mind..."

"No, Georgie. It's not Tuesday. I need to talk to you. It's important. It's about the old days."

The women playing mahjong with Georgette glowered at Gloria. They looked to Georgette for guidance. The identity of the table's queen bee was no mystery.

Georgette frowned and jerked her head to the right. The universal symbol for *beat it.*

The women stood from their seats and wandered off, eyeing Gloria, no doubt wondering what made her so *special.*

Gloria scowled back at one persistent gawker and slid into the now empty seat beside Georgette.

"I think that one cheats."

Georgette laughed. "Gloria, you think everyone eez up to something."

"Everyone is."

"What can I do for you? What has you in a tizzy?"

Gloria pulled her glare from the mahjong cheater who'd perched nearby.

"First, how are you, Georgette?"

Georgette shrugged. "Bon. I've been more out of breath lately. Zey had to give me oxygen once."

"I told you, you should've quit smoking sooner."

"Gloria, I am French."

Gloria nodded. It was true.

Georgette tapped Gloria's arm. "So tell me your problem."

"I have a question for you. Do you think your son was right to bring you here?"

Georgette's eyes blazed as if someone had jump-started her battery. "*No.* I should be at home with a private nurse—"

Georgette coughed and gasped for a breath. Gloria covered her friend's clenched fist with her hand to stop it from shaking.

"Take a breath, dear. Don't get yourself upset."

Georgette took several deep breaths. Her shoulders

relaxed. "I am sorry. You know how angry I am."

"I know. Unfortunately, it's your son I've come to talk to you about."

"What has he done now?"

"I think he's kidnapped a friend of mine."

"What?"

"Remember the man I told you I'd been passing during my walks?"

"Zee one with zee funny tee shirts?'

"Yes. I hired a private investigator to find him. She says he's being held by your son."

"What? To what end? Why would Louis do such a thing?"

"From what she tells me, it sounds like your son is starting the family business up again."

"What?" Georgette slammed her fist on the table, sending the mahjong tiles dancing. Several rained to the floor and clattered on the hardwood. Gloria heard the cheater behind her moan, no doubt realizing their game wouldn't be continuing.

Gloria felt the corner of her mouth twitch. *Ha. That will teach that cheating wench to look at me.*

"This is unacceptable. I did too much. It took me too long—"

Gloria nodded, allowing Georgette time to vent.

"I'm wondering if Louis put you in here so you wouldn't meddle with his business." Gloria dropped her voice to a whisper.

"After he saw what it did to his father? I spent a decade unraveling this family from violence."

"I know. I know."

"It was nearly impossible—such were the alliances that had been made. Those awful men. They didn't want to lose Victor's organization. But I did it."

"And no sooner did you finish, than your son checked

you in here."

Georgette's lips pressed into a tight knot. "Ungrateful brat." A puzzled look crossed her expression. "Wait. Does your tee shirt friend deal?"

"Drugs? I don't know. I don't think so."

"Zen why would my son take him?"

"I don't know. I was hoping maybe you had some information that would give me some leverage with your son. I need to save Ryan."

"Who is Ryan?"

"That's my kidnapped suitor's name, Ryan Finnegan."

"Ryan Finnegan..." Georgette's gaze drifted toward the ceiling.

Gloria felt a pang of nerves. Georgette recognized the name. Maybe Ryan *was* some sort of old rival. Maybe he was a dealer...

"Zee name is so familiar..."

Gloria held her breath, giving Georgette time to collect her thoughts.

"Zee club!" Georgette thrust her index finger into the sky to punctuate her recollection.

"What's that?"

"Louis's club." Georgette shook her head and waved her hands before her, signifying she wanted to start over. "Victor had a building, far into the trees, where he kept *supplies*." Her voice dropped as she said the last word.

"Go on."

"I was going to sell the building, but Louis wanted to turn it into a nightclub. He had just turned twenty-one and his mind was very much on play. I thought maybe he could turn his passions into a business and agreed to let him try. I put one of my business managers in charge of helping him with the money and all was well for a while..."

"What happened?"

"A boy died. In the club. A young man. I recall his last name was Finnegan."

"How did he die?"

Georgette shrugged. "Who can say? Overdose they thought. I couldn't have my assets under such suspicion with our history. I forced Louis to close the club and sell the building."

"You think my Ryan is related to the boy who died?"

She nodded. "It makes sense, no?"

Gloria placed a hand on Georgette's.

"I've missed you. I haven't visited in a while."

Georgette grasped her hand. "I've missed you too my friend."

"We are friends aren't we?"

"But of course."

Gloria squeezed Georgette's hand a little tighter. "Great. So tell me...where would your son keep a prisoner?"

A silence fell nearly as fast as the smile from Georgette's face.

CHAPTER TWENTY-SIX

Seamus left the room as Charlotte and Declan stared at each other.

"I don't want this to be weird," said Declan.

Charlotte gaped. "You don't want this to be weird? *Everything* has been weird since you picked up a gun at Jackie's. What don't you want to be weird?"

"Everything. Nothing. I know a lot has happened in the last twenty-four hours and I don't want questions to fester."

Though she'd intended to try and stay angry a little longer, Charlotte couldn't help but laugh. "When have you ever known me to keep my mouth shut and fester?"

Declan threw his arms around her as if she'd just been rescued from living on a deserted island with a volleyball as her best friend.

"Ow...my shoulder..."

He shifted his arm. "Sorry."

She nestled between his pecs. "No biggie. Just my little ol' gunshot wound." Charlotte didn't consider herself a hugger, but now that he'd maneuvered away from her wound, she had *no* complaints. She wrapped her arms around his waist and he squeezed a little harder.

"I was afraid you were mad," he murmured into her hair.

"Well, I am mad, a little..."

He released her slowly and stared into her eyes. "Then let 'er rip. Hit me with any concerns."

She grimaced, organizing her thoughts. "I suppose I feel a little deceived because you've always been a little...uh...*effeminate* isn't the word—"

Declan's eyes widened. "*Effeminate?*"

"Poncy!" called Seamus from the back of the house.

Declan scowled. "She doesn't need your help, Seamus."

Charlotte's head tilted. "Actually, poncy's not bad..."

"I know. Okay. I'm not an *ape man like some people*," Declan yelled the last five words over Charlotte's head toward Seamus' room.

"You're more like the prep school-boy type," suggested Charlotte.

"Nerd!" screamed Seamus.

"Using a napkin when I eat doesn't make me a nerd!"

Charlotte held up her hands. "Okay, okay. I think we all get the idea."

Declan's nostrils were flaring as he stared in the direction Seamus had wandered. It was easier to imagine him in fatigues tromping through the jungles of Columbia when he wore that particular expression.

Charlotte put her hand on his chest and his attention returned to her. His expression softened.

"You get the idea," she said. "You've always had a sort of a nice-boy feel, and then I find out you were learning martial arts and shooting guns and it makes me feel like you were lying to me on some level. Not to mention when you filled me in on your history with Stephanie, you could have mentioned you ran through the jungles of South America together."

"You're right. I should have told you. I was just so young and stupid then. That wasn't me. It's so embarrassing—"

"You're only twenty-seven now."

"There's a big difference. For some of us." His gaze shot in Seamus's direction again. "I was in a bad place at the time. And while I enjoyed the training and the excitement of being in the field, I think it also helped me focus. It helped me realize soldiering wasn't what I wanted to do for a living. So I left."

"And Stephanie?"

Declan looked away. "She stayed. Let's just say it fit her better than it fit me."

"She shot those men at the club."

He nodded.

"You helped her hide the gun."

He shook his head. "I took her prints off it and tossed it back on the ground."

"Won't the cops think it's weird there's a gun with no prints?"

"When your choices are *evidence* and *no evidence*, always pick the latter. Not finding a gun would have been even stranger."

"Mariska and the other ladies saw Stephanie with that gun."

"Saw her with *a* gun. Do you think any of them can tell one from another? Plus they'll never think to ask about it. The police think drug dealers were the problem—not lawyers and old ladies."

Charlotte considered this. "Hopefully they won't look too closely into Darla. She's got a secret history like you."

Declan chuckled.

"Why wouldn't Stephanie take credit for killing the bad guy when he drove through the wall?"

"That gun shot the guy in the parking lot, too."

"Right. It might be harder to explain why, when and how she shot *him*."

Charlotte paced. "Stephanie doesn't want scrutiny."

Declan shook his head.

"Because she's a lawyer?"

Declan nodded.

"And a killer."

Declan stared.

"She is, isn't she?"

Declan's mouth hung open, as if he was unable to find the right way to start his response.

Charlotte tried again. "Okay, let me dial back a little. Let's assume she killed people while with the Honey Badgers, like any soldier might. My question is—is she killing *here*?"

"Well, two, yesterday—"

"One and a half. Pirro finished off the guy in the parking lot."

"True."

It hadn't been that long since Charlotte had discovered Stephanie's mother was a notorious serial killer. Had the apple not fallen far from the tree?

"Is she a serial killer like her mother?" she asked.

Declan grimaced. "No. I—No."

"You don't know?"

"I don't. I swear."

"But it isn't out of the realm of possibility?"

Declan took a deep breath. "I don't know."

Charlotte sat on the edge of the sofa. "I need to talk to Stephanie. Find out where Ryan is being held exactly."

"That's why I went to see her."

"Oh? Not because the first rule of Honey Badger club is that you don't talk about Honey Badger club?"

"No. Because I knew you needed more info about Ryan. I thought she might tell me."

"She must have been thrilled to find out you were there to help *me*."

"I told her I hoped she felt better soon, too."

"That was sweet."

"Thank you. She told me she saw Ryan in a back room at *Irony Dry Cleaning*. It was one of the investments Louis's mother made with their ill-gotten gains. Ryan was tied to a chair. His face had been a little rearranged."

"They were torturing him?"

"Sounded more like a standard beating."

"Oh, like the sort of standard beating the Honey Badgers used to dole out?"

"Is everything going to come back to my quasi-military history from now on?"

Charlotte nodded. "For a while."

"Fair enough."

Charlotte stared through the back sliding doors at the pool.

"Whatcha thinking about?" asked Declan, sitting in the chair across from her.

"I talked to Frank this morning, hoping he'd have information for me about Ryan. He said the cops did a sweep of the dry cleaners and found nothing."

"Hm. You think Stephanie was lying?"

"No. For once I don't. Why would she lie about seeing an old man tied to a chair?"

"Maybe he's important. You saw those photos on his phone. He wasn't acting like a normal, innocent guy hanging out watching drug dealers."

"True. I should know better to underestimate retirees. I have that phone in my purse. You just reminded me there were some voicemails on there I wanted to check."

Charlotte stood to retrieve her purse from the kitchen table where she'd left it. Declan took her hand.

"So we're cool?"

She nodded. "We're cool." Her gaze darted toward her purse. Declan noticed.

"Mostly because you just realized you have a case to work on and it's all you can think about now?" he asked.

She grinned, squinting one eye at him. "Maybe a *little*."

He chuckled and released her hand. "By all means...don't let me stop you."

In all the commotion following the attack on Jackie's, she'd forgotten to finish checking Ryan's phone for information. It was a miracle she'd remembered to plug it in again after returning from the police station.

She called up the voice mail as she walked back toward Declan.

"Mr. Finnegan, this is Rob from maintenance. Just wanted to let you know we'll be up there to fix your sink on Thursday."

"Anything?" asked Declan.

"A phone call from maintenance about his sink from two months ago."

"That seems useful. Put it on speaker."

She switched the phone to speaker for the next message. There was a beep and a second message played.

"Dad—it's Craig. Craziest thing...I think I saw Firehead..."

The message ended there with what sounded like nervous laughter. Charlotte felt her jaw creaking open as she listened. She played it a second time.

"Did he say *Firehead*?" asked Declan.

"It's hard to tell. It's garbled."

"Like he has a bad connection."

She nodded. "The date is the same day Craig died. This could have been his last message."

"You think he kept it for nostalgia?"

"Maybe..." Charlotte pulled her own phone from her purse and did an Internet search for *Craig Finnegan death.* She found a newspaper article and read through it.

"Didn't Jackie say her disco already had the bar when she moved in? It had already been a club?"

"Yes."

"And the building was owned by Georgette Enterprises?"

"Named after Louis's mom."

Charlotte held out her phone. "Guess where they found Craig Finnegan dead?"

Declan squinted at the screen. "At Jackie's club?"

"Not far from it. He was dead in his car of an apparent overdose."

"You think he was at that club?"

"He does sound a little giddy on the recording. Maybe he's drunk?"

"That nervous laughter at the end kind of gave me the chills. It's like he was afraid of Firehead and was relieved to be away from him..."

"I know what you mean—" Charlotte gasped. "Could he have meant a *redhead*?"

"You're thinking the guy who shot the man in the parking lot?"

"*Pirro*. Has to be, right? That's why Ryan was watching the crew on the corner. He's trying to find *Pirro*. Firehead."

Declan frowned. "And Pirro found him instead."

CHAPTER TWENTY-SEVEN

Gloria entered the *Irony Dry Cleaners*, nodding with appreciation. The building was enormous, an old one-level brick building converted into a dry cleaning mecca.

When Georgette detached her family's finances from the drug world, she certainly hadn't *returned* any of the money to the junkies and pill-heads. Now her ungrateful son owned the largest dry cleaning operation in the state.

A woman approached the counter.

"Pick up?"

"No. I'd like to see the owner."

"He isn't here."

"Are you sure? Mr. Beaumont? Louis?"

The woman shook her head. "He isn't here. Do you want to speak to Mr. Pirro?"

"Mr. Pirro?"

"He works with Mr. Louis."

Gloria considered the offer. Her goal was to find Ryan Finnegan. Maybe Mr. Pirro could take her on a tour of the premises and they would stumble on where Louis was holding Ryan. Worse case, maybe he could tell her where Louis was lurking. "Yes. I'll talk to Mr. Pirro."

The woman walked to a windowed office on the right side of the building. Gloria couldn't see anyone inside, but even over the machines she heard a man barking something. A body leaned forward and peered at her through one of the office's windows.

He stared, and Gloria blinked, certain her eyes were playing tricks. The man had dark skin, but his hair was bright, light red.

The man left the office pushing by the woman who had gone to gather him. She scurried away, disappearing into the bowels of the building.

The man looked furious. He pounded on the counter, his gaze locked on Gloria. "You want something?"

Gloria straightened, rising to her full height of four foot eleven.

"I'm looking for Louis Beaumont."

"He ain't here."

"Do you know where he is?"

"No."

"Are you Mr. Pirro?"

"Yeah."

"Oh. Well, I'm a friend of Louis's family. He was supposed to give me a tour of the premises today."

Pirro's expression suddenly changed from angry to quizzical. "Hey...do I know you?"

Gloria scowled. "I don't think so."

Pirro stared at her a moment longer. After a moment the tension in his posture snapped like an over-stretched rubber band and he grinned.

The man had an unfortunate face, and the effect was unnerving.

"What is it you wanted again?" asked Pirro.

Gloria wrapped her arms across her chest. "I..uh...nothing—"

"A tour. Right? I'll give you a tour."

Pirro pushed open the half door to allow her behind the counter and held out his hand to usher her through.

She eyed the door as if it were booby-trapped. "Are you sure? I could wait for Mr. Beaumont..."

"No trouble at all."

Gloria bit her lip. "Okay. I *did* drive all the way here..."

"Sure."

She walked through. "I need to see every room of this building."

The man chuckled. "Sure. Dallas!"

Another face appeared in the office window, and a tall, skinny, blond young man jogged over to meet them.

"Yeah?"

"Come with us. I'm giving this lady a tour."

Dallas scowled. "Huh?"

"Just come with us."

The boy shrugged.

Pirro strode toward the back of the building, weaving between workers busy pressing and sorting clothing. Gloria had to break into a trot to keep up with the men.

"I guess this is the main working floor?" she asked, trying to maintain appearance as a tourist.

Neither of her guides answered. The unbearable noise probably kept them from hearing her. Hopefully, there would be some quiet areas coming soon and she could try and probe for more information on where Ryan might be.

They exited through a door into the back of the building and walked down a hall. Gloria's ringing ears began to relax.

"How long has this place been operating?" she asked.

Pirro and Dallas remained silent.

Rude. If Louis wasn't such a little bastard to his mother, I'd tell him to fire these two. As it is, he gets what he deserves— terrible employees.

Pirro opened a door and they walked into a small room with little more in it than two chairs, a cardboard box with a deck of cards on it and a closet.

Annoyed by the lack of communication, Gloria was about to complain when something about the chairs caught her eye. Reddish-brown spatter stained the arm of the larger wooden chair. A smattering of cut zip ties lay on the floor beneath it.

Could someone have been tied to that chair?

"This time you don't let her go," said Pirro poking Dallas in the center of his chest.

Gloria felt her nerves flutter. "What—"

Appearing aggrieved by the scolding tone in his boss's voice, Dallas cut her off. "I told you, Pirro. Louis told me—"

Pirro whirled, his face contorted with rage, spittle flying from his mouth.

"I don't care what Louis told you. Who's in charge?"

Gloria clutched her purse to her chest and stumbled back. Her leg hit the chair and she reached back to catch herself on its back to keep from falling.

Dallas paled. "You."

Pirro's gaze shot to Gloria. She lowered her purse, puffing her chest as large as her fear-laden, shallow breaths would allow.

"Who do you think you are?" she asked.

He leered. "I know who *you* are. I saw you when I was following Ryan. You're the woman he wore the t-shirts for."

Gloria swallowed. "You let me out of here *immediately*."

Pirro laughed and left with only a last nod to Dallas.

Gloria's jaw fell. She looked at Dallas. "Young man, I don't know what you or that man think you're doing, but you need to let me go immediately."

Dallas shook his head. "I'm sorry ma'am. I'm going to have to ask you to sit in that chair."

Gloria glanced at the chair. "Is that where you tied Ryan?"

Dallas sighed.

CHAPTER TWENTY-EIGHT

Ryan parked behind the dry cleaning and hopped out of his car.

Closing his eyes, he took a deep breath and released it slowly.

Just have to stay cool a little bit longer.

Louis wasn't the man he thought he'd be. The voicemail his boy left him the night he died had been spotty, but he was *sure* the man responsible for Craig's death had red hair. *Looks like Firehead.* He'd told the police *Firehead* was a creature he'd invented as a bedtime story for his son—a shadowy creature with fire for hair—but they didn't believe there was a connection. His death had been ruled an accidental overdose and the cops had moved on.

Only he was left to avenge his son. He'd traced ownership of the club near where they found Craig's body to Victor Beaumont's Georgette Enterprises.

He'd discovered that remnants of Victor's drug empire had survived his death. He'd started watching the corners, tracing the players. No one looked like Firehead yet.

Though he hadn't enjoyed the beating, his kidnapping had brought him to the inner sanctum.

But still no Firehead.

He had a plan now.

Louis Beaumont didn't seem like a criminal mastermind. He might have been the boss in name, but there had to be more players. He just had to play along and hang out long enough to find Firehead.

Pumping his arms to give himself courage, Ryan strode across the dry cleaners parking lot to the front door.

The young lady at the counter winced. He'd forgotten about his mangled face. The swelling had gone down enough that he could again see through the affected eye, but he still looked like a car accident victim.

"I'm here to see Louis," he said, smiling in the hopes he'd seem less scary.

The girl rolled her eyes.

"He's still not here."

"Still?"

"A lady was just looking for him. He wasn't here then either."

"Oh, okay. Should I wait? We had a meeting this morning, though we didn't set an actual time—"

She held up an index finger. "Wait here for me?"

He nodded and thrust his hands in his pockets, rocking from toe to heel.

"You Ryan?"

Ryan turned to find a man standing behind the counter near the swinging door that separated the retail and work areas.

Firehead.

The man had dark skin, he guessed a very tan Latino, but his hair was light red. Stunned, he forgot to answer and the man repeated his question.

"I said, *are you Ryan*?"

"Oh, yes. Hi." Ryan thrust out a hand. "And you are?"

"Pirro."

Pirro didn't raise his hand and after an awkward moment, Ryan let his drop.

"Is Louis here?"

"Louis asked me to take you back to the office when you got here."

"Great. Sounds good. Lead the way."

Pirro opened the door and Ryan followed him through the workers, retracing his steps from the previous day. Heading back into the belly of the building, his steps slowed.

Calm down. You found him. Just get a little more information.

Leaving the noise of the work floor behind, Pirro led Ryan down a hallway and opened a door. Ryan recognized it as the room in which he'd been held the day before.

"In *there?*" he said, stopping ten feet from where Pirro stood. He couldn't be sure, but it felt as though the right side of his face throbbed just being near that room.

"You need to wait," said Pirro, attempting what Ryan guessed was a smile.

You killed my son. I know you did.

Ryan pushed on. He rounded the corner into the room.

His old chair wasn't empty.

A small woman sat in the wooden seat he'd once occupied, her arms tied to the armrests as his had been. The woman hadn't been beaten, that he could see, but someone had tied a shirt sleeve around her face as a makeshift gag.

He recognized her immediately.

The woman from my walk. The woman I've been seducing with t-shirts.

In the twin chair sat Dallas, looking sheepish.

Ryan turned to face Pirro. "What is this?"

Pirro held a gun pointed at Ryan's belly.

"Sit down."

Dallas stood and stepped out of the way.

Ryan glanced from Dallas to Pirro and back again. He couldn't take them both. Certainly not when one had a gun and the woman sat tied to a chair, helpless to defend herself.

He sat in the other chair expecting Dallas would tie him as well. Dallas didn't move.

Pirro put his gun back in his waistband. "Dallas told me you were going to look at the books for Louis."

Ryan remained silent. Frustration and rage roiled inside his brain. He'd found the man who killed Craig. All his planning. All his work—

Pirro leaned against the wall appearing pleased with himself. "You think I don't know you. I know all about you. Once you start following my men, you're *asking* me to know all about you. That isn't something you should want."

Ryan remained silent and Pirro continued.

"You're that kid's father. The stupid kid who saw what he shouldn't have seen at the club."

Ryan jumped to his feet and Pirro raised his gun.

"Sit *down*."

Fists clenched, Ryan lowered into his seat.

"You're not here for the books. You came looking for me, didn't you?"

Ryan's teeth gritted until he thought they would crack.

Pirro laughed. "Now you're going to help me with the books, Daddy. You're going to tell Louis everything is cool."

Ryan found his voice. "Why would I help the man who killed my son?"

"Because if you don't, this lady is dead."

Ryan glanced at the gagged woman. Her eyes were teary and full of panic.

This is not how I planned our first date.

"Do you understand me? Don't bother telling me you hardly know her. You refuse, and she dies, and you die either way."

Ryan nodded.

"Louis is going to be here soon. He's going to think you're helping him. *You're helping me.* Remember that or she's dead. Got it?"

"Got it."

"Hey!" a voice echoed from the hall.

Pirro tilted back to see who approached. "Hey Louis."

Pirro shot Ryan one final glare as Louis appeared in the doorway.

"Ryan, you came back. I—" Louis's gaze fell on the gagged woman. He looked at Pirro. "What the—"

"It's a present for you, boss."

"A present?"

"Dallas told me you were going to have this guy look at the books."

"I—yeah, I thought—he's like an accounting genius. He's going to help us cook the books, so to speak."

Pirro cocked an eyebrow. "Yeah? You don't think I'm doing a good job?"

"What? No. No it's not that. It's just—you know. You're not an accountant. And I've got the dry cleaning and whatnot. It's a lot for one person. You have enough on your plate, too."

Ryan watched Louis fidget. He'd been right. Louis was the figurehead with the built-in money-laundering component. His last name opened doors in the narcotics community and his dry cleaning could easily launder money. Pirro needed him. Pirro had allowed the rich boy to think he was the boss, but he wasn't. Not by a long stretch.

Louis scratched at his cheek, staring at the woman.

"So who is she?"

"She's his girlfriend. We had to be sure he's legit, right? If he tries anything, he knows we have her."

"Right. Good thinking."

Louis stared at the dark-haired woman with what looked like regret.

Ryan did the math. There was no way Pirro would let him or the woman live. The thug was going to let him look at the books and declare them perfect to put Louis's mind at ease. Ryan knew the books wouldn't be perfect. They'd show just how much money Pirro had been stealing.

When he was done, Pirro would kill him and the woman.

He   couldn't   let   them   live.

CHAPTER TWENTY-NINE

"This is why I hadn't told you about the Honey Badgers yet, you know," said Declan as he parked his car down the block from *Irony Dry Cleaners.*

Charlotte unbuckled her seatbelt. "Why?"

"Because of your new vocation. You already take too many risks. I don't want you dragging me along and thinking you're invincible."

"Hm. Sort of full of yourself, aren't you?"

"That's not what I meant—"

Charlotte grinned and tapped his nose with her index finger. "Boop."

He sighed. "I boop your nose. You don't boop mine."

"But you're so adorable."

Charlotte hopped out of the car and the two of them walked towards *Irony.* She knew the cops said they'd already checked the building, but she couldn't shake the feeling that Stephanie had no reason to lie about seeing Ryan tied up there. Maybe they'd seen the cops coming. They weren't always subtle with their sirens and flashing lights. Maybe she and Declan could catch Louis and his men off guard.

The large, one-story brick building appeared quiet.

Though it possessed a counter and a glowing "Open" sign, she suspected in this more industrial part of town, this branch of *Irony* served more as a cleaning hub than a customer center.

As they grew closer, Charlotte spotted an alley running along the left side of the building, large enough for a car to enter.

"This looks like it leads to the back of the building."

"You don't just want to go in the front and tell them you came to pick up your old man?"

Charlotte chuckled. "I don't have my ticket."

They slipped down the alley and entered a fenced backyard largely consisting of dirt, cars and dumpsters. It appeared the employees used it for off-street parking.

Charlotte headed for the back door. She felt a hand grip her shoulder.

"Hold on there, Kojak. Let me go first."

Charlotte rolled her eyes. "I think I liked it better when you were hiding your past and let me take the lead."

"I never let you put yourself in danger just to keep my secret."

"You did a little."

"Did *not*. How about this. Did you bring a gun?"

Declan had caught her off-guard. Though she had the permit, she hadn't gotten used to the idea of carrying one.

"No. I haven't decided if I'm more of a Batman or a Punisher."

"Wow. Keeping your goals in check I see. You've gone from *you know, I think I might want to be a detective* to *I'm basically a superhero* in three months."

"I didn't say I'm a *superhero*, I just meant no-gun vs gun."

"But a hero, either way."

"Well sure, hey, here's an idea. Can we try and find Ryan please?"

She gave him a playful shove towards the door.

Declan crept up the short stairs to the windowless back door and tried the knob.

"Locked."

Charlotte grimaced. There were windows on either side of the door, but both hung too high to see through.

"If I stood on your shoulders, I could look in those windows."

"If you stood on my shoulders? What are we, a circus act now?"

"Come on. There has to be a way to do it. I'll take my shoes off. I know your main issue with the idea is getting footprints on your shirt."

"Very funny. Fine. But then we need to leave this to the police."

Charlotte offered a non-committal grunt and yanked off her sneakers as Declan took his position beneath the first window.

"How do we do this?" asked Charlotte.

"I'll squat down, you climb up and stand on my shoulders and use the wall to keep your balance. Then I'll stand and you walk yourself up the wall with your hands."

"So you're basically going to do squats with me on your shoulders."

"Just the one."

"Okay."

With a little trial and error, suppressing giggles, Charlotte managed to perch on Declan's shoulders.

"Ready?" he asked.

"Ready."

He stood and she worked her way up the brick wall with her palms to keep her balance as she rose.

"That was too fast," she said, nearly toppling.

"The slower I rise the harder it is. You're not one of those super petite girls, you know."

"Are you kidding? I'm like a tiny little flower—"

Charlotte cut short. The window had a shade over it, but it was torn. Through the hole, she could see a dark-haired woman sitting in a chair. She had a white shirt tied around her head. It looked as though her hands were bound to the arms of the chair. Charlotte squinted. On the woman's finger sat a large golden ring shaped like a frog.

Gloria.

How could Gloria be captured here too?

She gave the window a jerk and it opened easily. She thrust her top half through, hanging there while she tried to get the rest of herself in.

"Charlotte!" she heard Declan hiss beneath her.

Charlotte half-slithered and half-collapsed to the ground. Jumping to her feet, she searched for signs that someone had heard her. The room was empty but for Gloria, who'd heard the commotion of her entry and now strained to catch a glimpse.

Charlotte moved to her friend and pulled the makeshift shirt gag from her mouth.

"What are you doing here?" she asked. She'd never seen Gloria so distraught. Her cheeks were streaked with tears that had fallen as far as they could before being absorbed by the gag.

"Oh Charlotte, I'm so glad you're here. They're going to kill us."

"Us?"

"They have Ryan, too."

Charlotte plucked at Gloria's bindings, cursing to herself that she didn't carry a pocketknife of some sort. She made a mental note to add that to the list of things she needed to carry at all times. No wonder Batman wore a utility belt.

"I need to let Declan in. Stay here."

"Don't leave me!"

"I won't. Shh!"

Charlotte peeked through the room's only door into an empty hallway. To the left, she could see down to a windowed door. Through it, workers pressed clothes. To the right, she saw the door to the backyard. She tiptoed down the hall to unlock and open the door. Declan was there looking irritated.

"There you are. I didn't know if you'd crawled in the window or if someone had grabbed you."

"Sorry. I found Gloria."

"Gloria? Your client?"

Charlotte put her finger over her lips and motioned for him to follow her.

As they headed down the hall, a toilet flushed behind a door across from the room where Gloria sat.

Declan and Charlotte looked at each other. Charlotte scampered into the room with Declan on her heels and they shut the door.

"Declan, Gloria, my client. Gloria, this is Declan, my boyfriend."

"I think we met before," said Gloria.

"Okay, we'll do the social stuff later." Charlotte looked at Declan. "I need to get her untied. Do you have a knife?"

He shook his head.

"There's no way to get these zip-ties undone without scissors or something. I've tried to chew through them before. It's impossible."

Declan frowned. "Should I ask when you were in a position to chew through zip-ties?"

"I was just seeing if it could be done. It can't."

Declan shook his head. "I worry about you sometimes."

Gloria stomped her zip-tied little feet. "You have to hurry. Dallas will be back."

"Dallas?" She looked at Declan and knew they both suspected that's who they'd heard in the bathroom.

As if on cue, they heard a door open in the hallway and a man whistling.

"Here he comes," said Charlotte.

"Don't leave me here!" wailed Gloria.

The door began to open and Declan and Charlotte threw themselves against the wall behind it.

A skinny young man entered, fiddling with the leather belt that held up his baggy jeans. He looked up at Gloria.

"Hey, what happened to your gag—"

Declan reached past Charlotte and grabbed Dallas by his t-shirt with one hand, striking him hard in the face with his opposite fist.

Charlotte thought she saw Dallas's eyes cross as he slumped to the ground.

Charlotte and Declan stared at him. He didn't move.

"Did you *kill* him?" asked Charlotte.

Declan squatted beside the body, feeling for a pulse. "No. Glass jaw I guess. He's unconscious."

Charlotte shrugged. "That works. I need to get Gloria out of here."

"He has a knife in his pocket," said Gloria, nodding toward the motionless body. "I watched him pick his teeth with it. It's one of those *poppy* kind."

Charlotte squinted. "Poppy?"

Declan searched Dallas's pockets and retrieved a switch blade. He hit the release and the blade popped forth.

Charlotte nodded. "Ah. *Poppy.*"

Declan cut the zip-tie binding Gloria to the chair and helped her to her feet. "Let's go."

Charlotte put her hand on Declan's arm. "Gloria said Ryan is still here. She said they're going to kill him."

Declan scowled. "Don't even think about going after him. Call the police. We need to get her out while we can."

Charlotte nodded and retrieved her phone to dial 911 as

they made their way out the back door. By the time they'd reached Declan's car, they could hear sirens.

"They're coming," said Charlotte.

Declan helped Gloria into his back seat. The tiny woman was shaking.

"We should take her to the hospital."

Charlotte stared down the street in the direction of the dry cleaning. Just past that brick building, the nose of a car poked from an alley.

The hood had flames painted on it.

"That's Pirro's car," said Charlotte, pointing.

Declan followed her direction. The car pulled out of the alley and tore off away from the dry cleaning.

"He's getting away."

"You want me to chase him?" asked Declan.

"Yes—we don't have to catch him, but we can keep eyes on him."

Declan shook his head. "I don't know..." he mumbled, but he'd already pulled from the curb. They drove ten feet before a cop pulled in front of the dry cleaners, blocking their way. Declan attempted to circumvent the officer, but a mob of workers poured from the building, filling the streets and making it impossible to go anywhere without hitting someone.

"He got away," said Charlotte.

Declan put his car into park.

CHAPTER THIRTY

"You again," said Frank.

Charlotte grinned. "I told you I'd be coming by for an update."

An ambulance had arrived on scene at *Irony* to take Gloria in for a checkup. Other than some friction burns on her wrists and shot nerves, she seemed fine.

Declan needed to go back to work, so Charlotte dropped him off—promised she'd stay out of trouble—and borrowed his car to visit Frank, her direct hotline to the police. She needed to know if they'd caught Pirro.

Frank tapped his computer keyboard to spring the darkened screen to life. "Yeah, yeah. I called them for you. They found that car with all the flames and plaid you told them about."

Charlotte perked. "They did? Did they find Ryan? He wasn't in the building. Pirro must have taken him hostage."

Frank shook his head. "No people, just the car."

Charlotte slumped. "Where'd they find it?"

"Out off of route sixty. Not far from Jackie's disco."

"How could they just disappear?"

Frank shrugged. "If it makes you feel any better, from

what I understand there were two sets of footprints, but they lost them in the swamp."

Charlotte stared at the floor, thinking.

"You look like you just lost your best friend," said Frank.

"Pirro must have taken Ryan to be sure he had leverage in case the cops had him cornered. But now that he's free, there's no reason for him not to kill his hostage."

"They didn't find a body. That's a good sign, right?'

"I suppose. I'll get out of your hair. Thanks again."

"No problem. Hey, good work finding Gloria."

"Thanks. Tell me if you hear anything about Ryan."

Frank nodded. "I will."

Charlotte returned to Declan's car and pointed it in the direction of his shop. She was nearly there when she found herself making a U-turn and heading toward Jackie's club.

Why would Pirro head right for the swamp?

There had to be a hideout there she'd missed. He wouldn't return to Jackie's club. That wouldn't make any sense.

Something was eating at her.

The pipeline they'd followed to escape their own personal disco-Alamo had a hatch that popped up in the middle of the swamp.

Could he have headed for that?

No. There wasn't any reason to try for that entry point. First, it was locked from the inside—she'd made sure of that— and the only other place it lead was—

The diner.

That's what's eating at me.

Mariska said the diner hadn't had any pie. There'd been a kitchen, but no food. There *had* been some men sitting in the dining area having coffee...

She recalled the map Jackie had found in her parking lot and the half-hearted second pipeline leading from what turned out to be the diner.

What if it wasn't a diner at all. What if it was a *pretend* diner, serving as a nexus between pipelines. A popping out point.

If Jackie's club had been the warehouse, maybe the diner served as the pickup spot for distribution, a spot where they could supply dealers without revealing the location of their warehouse.

And if there was a second pipeline leading from the diner, where would it go?

Warehouse, distribution center...

Safe house.

They needed a safe house. Stash houses and warehouses could be discovered and raided. They needed a safe place to hide if things went bad.

Wouldn't that be where Pirro would go?

Charlotte hit the gas. She needed to find the entrance to the second pipeline. It would lead her to the safe house.

It would lead her to Ryan.

CHAPTER THIRTY-ONE

Stephanie's chest hurt. The operation had gone well, her lung had been inflated like a beach ball, but everything *hurt*.

It had been a terrible twenty-four hours.

First I forget my gun, then I get shot...

It was like she'd never even killed someone before.

She wasn't sure how much longer she could lie in bed. There was no way she'd be eating hospital food, so they'd have to set her free or watch her wither away and die of starvation.

There was a thud on the door of her room and she watched it shudder. It opened six inches, and a face, about waist-high, appeared.

An angry old woman muttered beneath her breath.

"Will you give me a push, Ruslan?"

A young man appeared above and behind the woman. He opened the door wide enough to roll the wheelchair-bound woman into the room.

Stephanie recognized the young man. He was Louis's flunky, the boy who'd popped his head into the room during her last meeting in Louis's office.

"What are you doing here?' asked Stephanie. It still hurt a little to talk.

Ruslan nodded toward the old woman as he parked her beside the bed.

Stephanie lowered her view to focus on the old woman. She had an impressive coif of dark hair and a determined glare she used to hold Stephanie's attention before speaking.

"I need you to earn your million."

Stephanie arched an eyebrow. "My million?"

"My son offered you a million dollars to wipe out his rival."

Stephanie pictured the photograph she'd seen in Louis's mother's bedroom. The woman posing with her husband was considerably younger in that image, but Stephanie could see the similarities. She also detected the touch of a French accent.

"You're Georgette? I thought Louis put you away in a home."

Georgette smirked. "You're charming."

Stephanie chuckled, stopping when the pain started.

"Do you want to know who eez rival eez?" asked Georgette.

Stephanie licked her lips. Lying in her hospital bed with nothing else to do, she thought she'd pieced together the identity of her target. She felt stupid, not having realized it sooner.

She smoothed her blanket. "Let's assume I know what you're talking about."

Georgette nodded. "Let's."

"Good. Now, if I were an assassin, hired by your son to kill his rival, I would guess the mystery man was..." Stephanie looked at the tall young man standing against the wall behind Georgette. "Can I get a drumroll?"

Ruslan's eyes widened. "Me?"

"Who else?"

He glanced at Georgette. She didn't turn to give him any indication of her feelings on the topic, so he stuck out his index fingers and pretended to drum while fluttering his tongue to approximate the rhythm.

"Thththththththththth..."

Stephanie held up her right hand—holding aloft her left hurt too much—and made her announcement with flair. "Pirro!"

The drumroll ceased.

Georgette's expression didn't change.

Stephanie frowned. "*Pirro.* Right? He's pretending to help Louis while building a gang of his own?"

"Wouldn't 'ee have killed you when you started snuffing his underbosses?"

Stephanie shrugged with her right shoulder. "He did. I mean, he tried to."

"And then?"

"And *then*?"

"'Ee didn't try again?"

"Aah...no." Stephanie pouted. The old broad had a good point. "I figured he was too afraid Louis would be mad at the news of my death?"

Georgette laughed, coughed, and then laughed again. "Have you met my son?"

"Yes. I—"

"Do you think Pirro would *ever* worry about disappointing Louis? Of losing control over him?"

Stephanie sighed. "I guess not."

"Why?"

"Because your son is a schmuck. No offense."

"None taken. You're right. Eez an idiot. But eez *my* idiot. Which is why I always keep eyes on him."

Stephanie and the young man exchanged a glance.

"So you had spies."

Georgette jerked a thumb in the boy's direction. "Ruslan is on loan from a Russian business associate of mine."

"So you know about me. And you know Pirro is using Louis."

Georgette nodded.

"But Pirro isn't his rival on the streets. Pirro genuinely *wanted* me to wipe out the rival leader and his crew?"

Georgette nodded.

"But that man waiting to kill me—only Louis and Pirro knew—"

Georgette used her eyes to point at Ruslan behind her. "You suspected a mole, perhaps?"

Stephanie glanced at the boy. *The mole.*

She stared, wide-eyed at Georgette.

"*You*? His mommy is the rival drug lord?"

"I'm the *only* drug lord."

"But he had you committed to a home."

Georgette shrugged. "Eet's not like I need to stand on the corners myself. And where could I be less conspicuous?" Georgette coughed. "I also own the place and I'm dying of lung cancer, so it isn't a bad place to be. I've grown very good at mahjong."

"I haven't learned to play that yet."

"It's fun."

"I'll check it out." Stephanie had a thought. "Oh *no*. I owe you an apology."

"For what?"

"The finger wreath..."

Georgette grunted. "Hm. Yes. That was unfortunate. They were some of my best men."

"Not the one who tried to kill me. He was terrible."

"True. I underestimated you."

"Because I'm a girl?"

"Because my idiot son hired you."

"Ah. Good point. So, where do we stand?"

Georgette sighed. "After I appeared to go legit, I tried to

steer Louis away from the, uh...family business. It didn't work. When I realized the little twit was bound and determined to follow in his father's footsteps, I hired Pirro to be his second-in-command and keep him out of trouble."

"Why didn't you let him work under you?"

"Ee doesn't listen to me. Plus, ee'd get himself caught and blow my cover. It took me a decade to make eet look like the family had gone straight. Ee'd have destroyed everything in the time eet takes him to finish one level of his stupid video game."

"Fair enough. So Pirro got power-hungry?"

Georgette nodded. "It was only a matter of time before he killed my boy and me as well. When I heard about you, yes, I tried to have you killed at first—but then I thought you might come in handy, especially after you killed my captain."

"Again, sorry about that."

"I meant to approach you before you got to my *second* captain, but my health took a bit of a bad turn and things happened too fast."

"Again, I'm *so* embarrassed. The wreath—"

Georgette waved her away. "Water under zee bridge."

Stephanie realized the old woman might be able to answer a question she'd had for a while. "Hey, what's up with Pirro's hair?"

"His mother told him his father had been a Scottish business man."

"He *is* tall for a Columbian."

"He became obsessed with the Scots. Rumor is heez seen *Braveheart* over a hundred times. Screams *Freedom!* every time he's excited or wants to leave."

"Huh."

They fell silent while Georgette dug for a tissue and coughed into it. When she'd caught her breath, Stephanie continued following the old woman's logic.

"So to earn my million, I need to kill Pirro?"

Georgette nodded. "Yes. But there eez a catch."

"What's that?"

"I need you to do it *now*."

Stephanie gaped. "Now? I just had my lung inflated."

"I need to extract Louis from a situation right now and I can't have Pirro loose. That weasel is headed toward our safe house. He's without his men and he won't be expecting you."

Wincing, Stephanie sat up and swung her legs over the side of the bed. Her chest throbbed in time with her heartbeat.

This is going to be difficult, but not impossible.

"Fine. But I want a two hundred and fifty thousand dollar bump."

"For what?"

"For having the strength and will to pull this off in my condition."

Georgette laughed. "You wanna talk strength and will?"

The old woman's voice suddenly sounded very different. Stephanie pushed aside her pain and looked up to find Georgette smiling.

"Girly, I'll show you *strength and will.* I've been copping this stupid French accent for fifty-five years. I'm from the *Bronx.*"

CHAPTER THIRTY-TWO

As Charlotte drove to the swamp diner she decided it *might* be a good idea to carry a gun in the future. The deeper she drove into swampland, the more reckless looking for the second pipeline on her own seemed.

I should have asked my boyfriend, Jean Claude-VanDeclan, to join me.

No. He would have tried to talk her out of it. Or insisted she bring an army of police, and she knew the police wouldn't jump to action based on her hunch about a second pipeline leading to an imaginary safe house. Showing them a map that looked like a first grade project wouldn't help.

Maybe Frank would have come, but he gets so cranky...

Charlotte stepped out of the car and fished a flashlight from her trunk. She took a deep breath. Mariska had called the building a diner, but it didn't have a name across the front. Just crime tape. Maybe it wasn't supposed to be a diner and only looked like one from the inside. Maybe it wasn't all that *odd* it had no pie. Maybe Mariska had just really *wanted pie.*

Okay. Let's go. I'll be fine.

Charlotte knew there was a phone in the little building—Declan had used it to call the cops after escaping the tunnel.

She'd locate the second tunnel, maybe scoot down it to see what was on the other side, and if she had no cell signal there, she'd run back down the tunnel and call the police.

Easy peasy.

She peeled back the tape and found the door unlocked.

Handy.

She poked her head inside.

"Hello?"

Nothing.

So far so good.

If the map was correct—and it had been so far—the pipeline would lead from the right side of the building.

Tables, chairs and a counter top claimed most of the space in the building's front room. It did look suspiciously like a little diner. The right side of the room had windows though, so she doubted it could be hiding access to the pipeline.

She walked through swinging doors to the back. A barren kitchen occupied the space, sans utensils and grease. More crime tape covered a hole in the far wall. It looked as though someone had opened a door through a thin piece of paneling, which had peeled away and knocked over a stack of orange crates.

Or maybe Declan had karate-chopped through it. Who knew anymore?

Charlotte turned to her right to find a walk-in freezer. She jerked open the door and found it cold but empty inside.

I guess drug dealers don't sweat their electric bills.

She couldn't help but think how offended the residents of Pineapple Port would be by this waste of air-conditioning. She'd once heard a lady say the worst part about menopause was the hot flashes, not for the discomfort, but for the extra air-conditioning bills.

Something about the freezer felt wonky. Charlotte stuck her head outside to check around the corner of the unit and then looked inside again.

It was shallow. The freezer didn't run as deep as the rest of the room.

The pipeline had to be behind the back wall of the freezer. She tapped on it.

It sounded hollow.

She was about to search for an axe when a large bolt in the center-top of the back panel caught her eye. There were circular scratch marks around it. On a whim she pushed on the metal panel and it swung to the left, just far enough to reveal an opening to a ladder that led down.

Bingo.

Flipping on her flashlight, she climbed onto the rungs leading into the second pipeline. Allowing the door to swing back into place, she saw it was possible to secure it on the opposite side. If someone was on the run they could disappear into the freezer, access the tunnel, and then secure the panel behind them. Then the people chasing them wouldn't be able to swing the wall aside and follow.

Charlotte walked as fast as she could down the pipeline without breaking into a trot. Just like the tunnel from Jackie's, this pipeline also possessed an escape hatch. She climbed up to take a look out, finding nothing but swamp.

She closed the hatch. A nervous thrill ran through her bones as she bolted it shut. She couldn't shake the feeling that if she didn't secure it quickly enough, thugs would throw open the hatch and grab her.

I'm scarred for life.

Luckily, sliding bolts through swamp hatches didn't come up that often.

She continued until she reached another ladder at the end of the tunnel. She climbed the rungs to a landing with a glowing red button.

This end of the tunnel is high tech.

She calculated the chances of the red button being a trap. It was hard to say. It didn't have a sign in blinking lights that said *PUSH!* pointing to it like a cartoon. That would have been suspicious.

She decided anyone using the tunnel to get to the safe house would be moving fast. They didn't want to fiddle with bolts. The bad guys had spent more money on the safe house door to make it easier to find safety should the need arise.

She took a deep breath.

She pushed the red button.

A clicking noise began to grind and she winced, covering her head with her hands.

The wall slid away.

She peered through her fingers and found herself facing a large, warehouse-like room. A small prop plane sat just inside the open hanger door to the right, and sunlight streamed into the building to reveal the most interesting part of the building.

The three people standing in the center of the room.

Six eyes swiveled in her direction.

Two belonged to Pirro, who held Ryan by the throat, the older man's head tucked in the crook of the redhead's arm.

Two, more wild, belonged to poor Ryan.

And two belonged to Stephanie, who stood three feet from the other two, a gun trained on Pirro. She wore light blue hospital scrubs. Her feet were bare.

Charlotte stood still, as if they couldn't see her unless she moved.

She heard Stephanie groan.

"Oh, *girlfriend.*"

CHAPTER THIRTY-THREE

Pirro swiveled his gun, which *had* been trained on Stephanie, and took a shot at Charlotte.

Somewhere in her locked brain, Charlotte had seen that coming, and had already bolted to the right toward the plane, hoping to hide behind it. At the time, it seemed like a better idea than dropping to the bottom of the tunnel below, but as the sound of a second gun exploded, she began to wonder.

Stephanie had fired. Blood spattered from Pirro's shoulder, forcing him to release Ryan. Free, Ryan roared, flailing at Pirro's gun.

Pirro fired again, but Ryan's interference ruined the thug's aim and a bullet struck high on the wall above Stephanie's head. Stephanie rolled away apparently unscathed but still yowling in what sounded like pain.

Pirro's gun skittered across the cement floor as he backhanded Ryan, connecting his balled fist with the side of the older man's skull. Ryan's head snapped back as he spun to the ground.

Pirro turned to locate Stephanie.

Seeing her chance, Charlotte ran toward Pirro's gun. Like a zombie refusing to die, Ryan bounced to his hands and knees and crawled to the gun at high speed, grabbing it before Charlotte could reach it.

"Everyone freeze!" shouted Ryan.

Nearly upon Ryan, Charlotte stopped and held up her hands, realizing he had no way of knowing whose side she was on.

On the other side of the room, Stephanie stood, gun in one hand, the other gripping the area beneath her left breast. She breathed in short, shallow gasps, her skin pale. Charlotte had never seen her so unraveled. Her hair looked like a raked haystack.

She wished she had a camera.

Pirro stood between Stephanie and Ryan, his hands held waist high, as if holding his hands over his head wouldn't be cool.

Ryan motioned to Charlotte to move from her position behind him. She accommodated without getting too close to Pirro.

Ryan shook the gun in Charlotte's direction. "Who are you?"

"My name is Charlotte. Gloria hired me to find you."

"Gloria?"

Charlotte realized Ryan and Gloria had never exchanged names. "The woman you wore the t-shirts for. The woman bound and gagged at the dry cleaners because she was so determined to find and save you."

The side of Ryan's lips curled into a smile. "Gloria," he repeated. The name seemed to please him. "She's okay?"

Charlotte nodded. "Just shaken up. She's very worried about you."

He nodded and turned his attention to Stephanie. "And you're here for Pirro. Why?"

Stephanie took a moment to compose herself, running her free hand through her hair. "He's been recalled by his employer."

"Recalled?"

Stephanie stared back at Ryan. Charlotte could feel the weight of that gaze.

"You're here to kill him," said Charlotte.

Ryan perked. "Is that true?"

Stephanie didn't answer.

Ryan trained his gun on Pirro. "That's why I'm here, too. He killed my son."

Pirro glowered. "Kid was in the wrong place. Nothing personal."

Ryan's hand shook as he held his weapon on his son's murderer. Charlotte had the impression he hadn't fired a gun before. Stephanie, who was standing almost directly behind Pirro, moved a few steps to the right to give Ryan a clear shot.

"Let me call the police," said Charlotte. "You don't have to kill him."

Ryan's jaw clenched, his index finger twitching on the trigger. "I don't know—I can't—"

Pirro huffed a laugh. "You haven't got the guts, old man."

Charlotte watched Ryan's hand tense.

"Ryan—"

"Let me take him," offered Stephanie.

Ryan's eyes shifted in her direction. "*I* should do it. He was my son."

Stephanie shook her head. "You have done it. You found him. You got your answers. You don't have to pull the trigger. You're the scales of justice, not the executioner."

Charlotte blinked at Stephanie.

That sounded almost poetic.

Ryan swallowed, head nodding, building momentum.

"Take him," he said.

Stephanie pointed her weapon at Pirro, walking towards him without hesitation.

Charlotte balled her fists. "*No.* I'm not going to stand here while you murder that man. I'll call the police."

She reached for her phone and Ryan trained his gun on her.

Charlotte lifted her hands back into the air. "Ryan—"

"She's taking him," he said.

"But whoever she's taking him to will kill him."

Ryan looked at Stephanie. "You're just taking him to be punished, right? He'll end up in jail?"

Stephanie smiled. "Sure. Jail."

She winked.

Charlotte's hands flopped to her sides. "Oh come on, Ryan, you know she's going to kill him. She's—she's a Honey Badger!"

Ryan sniffed. "She's the Rubia."

Stephanie shoved Pirro in the back with her gun. "Move it."

Pirro snarled and started forward.

"You're both dead," he said, running his finger across his own throat.

Stephanie shoved him again and they walked out of the hanger.

Charlotte looked at Ryan. "What's to keep me from telling everyone? Are you going to kill me?"

Ryan watched Stephanie disappear from view and lowered his gun.

"I'm not going to kill you. Are you going to send me to jail for letting my son's killer walk out of here with a pretty girl?"

A car engine roared to life and the two of them watched Stephanie's red viper appear at the entrance to the hanger. Stephanie's window lowered. She waved.

The sound of a muffled voice drifted from the vicinity of her trunk.

"FREEDOM!"

EPILOGUE

"I see you're wearing your big pink yes," said Charlotte, holding up her cocktail in cheers.

Gloria had invited everyone to her beach house to celebrate finding Ryan. She'd worn her answer t-shirt, the word *Yes* spelled out in pink marker across her chest. Ryan stood beaming at her side. They made a beautiful couple.

Gloria beamed. "It was the least I could do. You did an amazing job finding Ryan and saving my life."

"She saved mine, too," added Ryan, holding up his glass.

Charlotte and Ryan exchanged a knowing glance. Though she'd been determined to tell the police about Stephanie and Pirro, in the end Ryan refused to support her story. If he denied seeing Stephanie at the hanger, she'd sound like a loon. The idea of putting a grieving father in jail for aiding the assassin who rid the world of his son's killer, didn't warm her heart either.

She'd decided to take her win with Gloria and worry about Stephanie's nefarious secret life another day.

Gloria swept her hand to the left, her giant gold frog ring sparkling. "Charlotte, have you met my friend, Georgette Beaumont?"

A pretty, older woman in a wheelchair looked up at the sound of her name.

"Nice to meet you, Mrs. Beaumont," said Charlotte.

Georgette shook her hand. "Please, call me Georgette. Theeze is my son, Louis."

Charlotte surveyed the man standing behind Georgette's chair. He looked up from where he'd been staring at his own feet and nodded, his hands thrust deep into the pockets of his khaki shorts. He was handsome by the numbers, but looked as though the air had been let out of him.

His mother flung back her hand, catching him in the abdomen.

"Say hello like a *man*," she snapped.

Louis rolled his eyes. "Hello."

Charlotte nodded. "Hello."

The sensational story of how a man named Domingo "Pirro" Rodríguez, with deep ties to a Columbian drug cartel, had forced Louis Beaumont to use his late father's reputation in the drug world, had been all over the news the last week.

Charlotte had to believe there was some truth to the stories. Louis didn't look like a drug lord. He looked like a miserable child who'd been dragged to an adult party by his mother.

No one had come forward to refute Louis's claims that he was a victim, and it appeared he'd walk away from any involvement in the drug trade with a slap on the wrist.

Pirro wouldn't say different.

If Pirro ever showed up.

~~ THE END ~~

WANT SOME MORE? FREE PREVIEW!

If you liked this book, read on for a preview of the next Pineapple Port Mystery AND the Shee McQueen Mystery-Thriller Series (which shares characters with the Pineapple Port world!)

THANK YOU!

Thank you for reading! If you enjoyed this book, please swing back to Amazon and leave me a review — even short reviews help authors like me find new fans!

GET A FREE STORY

Find out about Amy's latest releases and get a free story by joining her newsletter! http://www.AmyVansant.com

ABOUT THE AUTHOR

USA Today and Wall Street Journal bestselling author Amy Vansant has written over 20 books, including the fun, thrilling Shee McQueen series, the rollicking, twisty Pineapple Port Mysteries, and the action-packed Kilty urban fantasies. Throw in a couple romances and a YA fantasy for her nieces...

Amy specializes in fun, exciting reads with plenty of laughs and action -- she tried to write serious books, but they always ended up full of jokes, so she gave up.

Amy lives in Jupiter, Florida with her muse/husband a goony Bordoodle named Archer.

BOOKS BY AMY VANSANT

Pineapple Port Mysteries
Funny, clean & full of unforgettable characters
Shee McQueen Mystery-Thrillers
Action-packed, fun romantic mystery-thrillers
Kilty Urban Fantasy/Romantic Suspense
Action-packed romantic suspense/urban fantasy
Slightly Romantic Comedies
Classic romantic romps
The Magicatory
Middle-grade fantasy

FREE PREVIEW

PINEAPPLE

GINGERBREAD MEN

A Pineapple Port Mystery: Book Seven –
By Amy Vansant

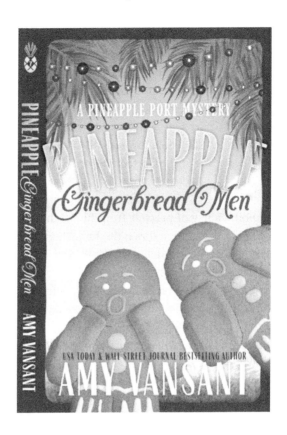

CHAPTER ONE

Kristopher Rudolph poured himself another bourbon as the

dog in his bathroom launched into its fifteenth chorus of *Yap Yourself a Merry Little Christmas*. The miserable little rat-creature would not *shut up*. He heard it trying to scratch a hole through the door and grunted, pleased he had no intention of trying to recover his damage deposit anyway.

The worst part was the noise. It sounded more like the dog was trying to dig a hole through his *skull* than the door.

How a dog the size of a football could make that kind of racket—

"Shut up!"

Grabbing a bag of pretzels from his kitchen counter, Kris tore it open and pounded down the hall. He cracked open the bathroom door and used his ankle to block the tiny dog's escape as he slipped in his hand, inverted the bag and shook it.

Pretzels rained. Startled, the Yorkshire terrier backed away from the door, looking like a long-haired toupee with eyes.

Kris glared at it. "There, you happy? You are going home tomorrow. I *promise*."

He shut the door.

Silence.

Well, *munching*, but that was better than barking.

Kris took a deep breath and patted his round tummy, suddenly craving pretzels. He strode back up the hall, shoved the empty pretzel bag into the kitchen garbage, grabbed a bourbon, and toted it to his overstuffed chair to park himself in front of the television. As a commercial for reverse mortgages blared, his gaze swept over his living room decorations.

Strips of lights lined the ceiling like disco crown molding. A Christmas tree stood beside him, blinking with frenetic urgency—middle section, bottom section, top section—over and over, sending semaphore messages to the reindeer, sleighs and giant snowmen flashing their own secrets from his front yard. A full set of reindeer ran across the wall above his sofa. Rudolph led the way. At least fifty other Rudolphs grinned from table tops and tissue box cozies.

He groaned and took a sip of his bourbon. "Freakin' Christmas."

Thanks to his last name, people around the little swamp-town he currently called home were always gifting him Rudolphs, thinking they were clever.

The presents were about as clever as sending someone from Maine a lobster mug.

I should be happy. Celebrating.

He took another sip of his bourbon and tried to concentrate on his upcoming retirement.

Somewhere warm. Somewhere they've never heard of Christmas. Somewhere they've never even heard of December.

Perched on at least six other flat surfaces, tiny stuffed elves stared at him with disapproving sideward glances, their arms crossed over their knees.

Kris winked at one as he sipped his drink. "Yeah, yeah, I've been naughty."

His shoulder muscles had just begun to unbunch when his doorbell rang and Jingle Bells sang throughout the house.

The dog began to bark anew.

Kris closed his eyes, searching for strength. Not only did he have to answer the door, but he had to pretend he enjoyed the company.

One more month and this hell will be over.

Setting down his bourbon, he stood and opened the front door.

Crowded in his doorway stood two poofy gingerbread men. Leaning to the left and tilting his head to the side, he found two more behind the first pair. He recognized the costumes from the Charity Christmas parade earlier that day. The gingerbread men had been running around, as gingerbread men were wont to do. The curious part was *he* organized the parade and *he* hadn't booked any gingerbread men. At the time he hadn't thought much about it. It wasn't unusual for people wearing silly costumes to join in a parade, unannounced. Especially in these Podunk little towns where half the locals' bloodlines intersected. But he had to admit, now that the cookies were standing on his doorstep, his curiosity had piqued.

He pulled at his enormous white beard and did his best to look jolly.

"My, my, look at you all. How can I help you?"

The foremost gingerbread shoved him with two caramel-colored mitted hands. Unprepared, Kris stumbled backwards, hands flailing to regain his balance. Bourbon splashed across the wall and his glass sailed through the air.

"We want what we're owed," said one of the cookies as they piled into his house. He couldn't tell which one. Their mouths didn't move.

CHAPTER TWO

Earlier That Day

"Ooh! Here come those little cars," said Mariska, pointing.

Older men, each with a red fez on his head, appeared driving tiny orange cars, weaving back and forth across the parade route as if the vehicles themselves had spent the day drinking.

Darla scowled. "Who are they? What do little cars have to do with Christmas?"

"They're Shriners. It's a club for men."

"What isn't?" muttered Darla.

Charlotte chuckled and looked at her watch. It was nearly Christmas and she had a lot to do. Back at her house an enormous embroidery machine waited patiently in her shed, eager to stitch Schnauzers and Cavalier King Charles Spaniels on golf head covers and polo shirts. Helping Mariska's son and daughter-in-law with their pet embroidery business had once been Charlotte's only job.

Now, she was officially a private investigator.

But with the holidays rapidly approaching, the crimes

had dwindled and the demand for Dachshunds on kitchen towels had gone up, and she'd agreed to help for one last holiday.

She glanced at the two older ladies beside her.

That is, if Mariska ever lets me get any work done.

Charlotte's adoptive mother had *insisted* she come watch the parade. After she'd been orphaned as a girl, Mariska, her husband Bob and Darla—with the help of Darla's husband Sheriff Frank—had arranged it so Charlotte could grow up in their fifty-five plus community, Pineapple Port. If it hadn't been for them, after the death of her grandmother, Charlotte would have been whisked off as a ward of the state. Shuffled through the system, she would have had a very different upbringing.

As it was, picking up some of their 'retiree habits' way too young was the worst that had happened to her. Most twenty-seven-year-olds didn't go to water aerobics or watch television with the closed-captioning on.

She had work to do and Mariska had insisted she go to a parade. *Oh well.* In the grand scheme of things, it seemed like a small price to pay.

"Why do we have a parade again?" she asked over the pounding of a local high school's marching band. There hadn't been a Christmas parade in Charity, the city that housed Pineapple Port, since she was a little girl.

"You can thank Kristopher Rudolph. The man who looks like Santa," called back Mariska.

Charlotte's brow knit as she pictured the man. Whenever she'd seen him she couldn't help but think his big white beard made for a poor facial hair choice in steamy Florida. It made her scratch her chin just thinking about it. "When did he move to Pineapple Port? Last summer, right?"

Mariska nodded, her auburn curls bouncing. "This is what he does. He arranges big Christmas events for towns to help them raise money for charity."

"The man is *obsessed*," chimed in Darla. "I had to deliver a cake to him for his charity bake sale and his house looks like this whole parade just marched right in there and took a seat."

Charlotte shrugged. "I guess with a name like Kristopher Rudolph..."

"I know *three* women who bought him Rudolph the red-nosed reindeer statues," said Mariska as four gingerbread men ran by, slapping kids' outstretched hands with their own puffy mitts. "They put no thought at all into it."

Darla hooked a thumb in Mariska's direction. "She took him a homemade jar of *Rudolph the Red Pepper Jelly.*"

Mariska nodded. "*That* was clever. Man needs another statue like he needs another whisker in his beard."

Darla winked at Charlotte. "Kris is single and he likes fruit cake. The ladies in Pineapple Port have been waiting *years* for a man like that to show up."

Mariska's eyes flashed. "I wasn't *flirting* with him."

"Not you. *You* just have way too much homemade pepper jelly in your cabinets."

Mariska's expression relaxed and she giggled. "I do. It's true. I think we overdid it this year."

Mariska gasped and pointed, nearly taking out the eye of the woman next to her. "There he is now."

With the blaring of sirens, a fire truck inched down main street, a jolly Santa perched on top, waving. Teenage girls dressed like elves grabbed handfuls of candy from red and green buckets and tossed treats into the crowd.

Charlotte looked at her watch again. "That's the end, right?"

"Of course it is. Santa's always last. Haven't you ever seen a Christmas parade before?"

"I grew up *here*, remember? I was about six the last time we had a Christmas parade."

"Don't be a Grinch. What are you in a hurry to get back to?"

"I have about twenty orders to stitch and Aggie Mae lost her Yorkie, Pudding. I promised I'd help her look for him."

Darla rolled her eyes. "That little thing's in a gator's belly by now. You'll notice there aren't a lot of packs of wild Yorkies roaming Florida. I'm surprised he lived this long."

Mariska smacked her friend's shoulder. "That's terrible."

Darla shrugged. "Terrible but true."

Get *Pineapple Gingerbread Men* on Amazon!

ANOTHER FREE PREVIEW!

THE GIRL WHO WANTS

A Shee McQueen Mystery-Thriller by Amy Vansant

CHAPTER ONE

Three Weeks Ago, Nashua, New Hampshire.

Shee realized her mistake the moment her feet left the grass.

He's enormous.

She'd watched him drop from the side window of the house. He landed four feet from where she stood, and still, her brain refused to register the warning signs. The nose, big and lumpy as breadfruit, the forehead some beach town could use as a jetty if they buried him to his neck...

His knees bent to absorb his weight and *her* brain thought, *got you.*

Her brain couldn't be bothered with simple math: *Giant, plus Shee, equals Pain.*

Instead, she jumped to tackle him, dangling airborne as his knees straightened and the *pet the rabbit* bastard stood to his full height.

Crap.

The math added up pretty quickly after that.

Hovering like Superman mid-flight, there wasn't much she could do to change her disastrous trajectory. She'd *felt* like a superhero when she left the ground. Now, she felt more like a Canada goose staring into the propellers of Captain Sully's Airbus A320.

She might take down the plane, but it was going to *hurt.*

Frankenjerk turned toward her at the same moment she

plowed into him. She clamped her arms around his waist like a little girl hugging a redwood. Lurch returned the embrace, twisting her to the ground. Her back hit the dirt and air burst from her lungs like a double shotgun blast.

Ow.

Wheezing, she punched upward, striking Beardless Hagrid in the throat.

That didn't go over well.

Grabbing her shoulder with one hand, Dickasaurus flipped her on her stomach like a sausage link, slipped his hand under her chin and pressed his forearm against her windpipe.

The only air she'd gulped before he cut her supply stank of damp armpit. He'd tucked her cranium in his arm crotch, much like the famous noggin-less horseman once held his severed head. Fireworks exploded in the dark behind her eyes.

That's when a thought occurred to her.

I haven't been home in fifteen years.

What if she died in Gigantor's armpit? Would her father even know?

Has it really been that long?

Flopping like a landed fish, she forced her assailant to adjust his hold and sucked a breath as she flipped on her back. Spittle glistened on his lips, his brow furrowed as if she'd asked him to read a paragraph of big-boy words.

His nostrils flared like the Holland Tunnel.

There's an idea.

Making a V with her fingers, Shee thrust upward, stabbing into his nose, straining to reach his tiny brain.

Goliath roared. Jerking back, he grabbed her arm to unplug her fingers from his nose socket. She whipped away her limb before he had a good grip, fearing he'd snap her bones with his Godzilla paws.

Kneeling before her, he clamped both hands over his face,

cursing as blood seeped from behind his fingers.

Shee's gaze didn't linger on that mess. Her focus fell to his crotch, hovering a foot above her feet, protected by nothing but a thin pair of oversized sweatpants.

Scrambled eggs, sir?

She kicked.

He howled.

Shee scuttled back like a crab, found her feet and snatched her gun from her side. The gun she should have pulled *before* trying to tackle the Empire State Building.

"Move a muscle and I'll aerate you," she said. She always liked that line.

The golem growled, but remained on the ground like a good dog, cradling his family jewels.

Shee's partner in this manhunt, a local cop easier on the eyes than he was useful, rounded the corner and drew his own weapon.

She smiled and holstered the gun he'd lent her. Unknowingly.

"Glad you could make it."

Her portion of the operation accomplished, she headed toward the car as more officers swarmed the scene.

"Shee, where are you going?" called the cop.

She stopped and turned.

"Home, I think."

His gaze dropped to her hip.

"Is that my gun?"

Get *The Girl Who Wants* on
Amazon!